ONLY THE STREETS TELL STORIES

First edition. January 26, 2024.

Copyright © 2024 Barry Robinson.

ISBN: 979-8224309887

Written by Barry Robinson.

I dedicate this book to my beautiful wife Fantha that has always been there for me through everything., to my mom, to my aunt Doris rest in peace, to my dad, to my brother Born and all his words of encouragement, to my cousin Kim who put in work for me to make this book possible, to Derrick Johns who showed me the way, and to my sons Lil Barry, Clayton and Corey, I pray you never give up on your dreams.

Only
The
Streets

Tell

Stories

By:
Barry Robinson

Chapter

1

Part

1

Laughing out loud from old memories. Telly could care less about the weird glances he got from the people at the crowded bus stop. He was finally free to do as he pleased. No more doing as he was told or doing something he didn't want to do. His so debt to society had been paid in full. Ten years to door.

Looking around the streets of North Philly, he was overwhelmed by the range of emotions he felt, Happy, sad, excited, scared, all at the same time. If his life depended on it, he couldn't describe in words what he was feeling at the moment. Though happiness seemed to overpower everything else. Ten years doing hard time taxed a heavy toll on a young man's heart, when he first fell down on his 3rd degree murder charge. He was a tall, skinny, nineteen-year-old black man running wild and out to get his props. Now, at the age of twenty-nine, six feet four, weighing two-hundred and forty pounds with solid muscle, he was no longer wild and could give a damn about props. His main concern at the moment was how he was going to survive electricity, shelter, clothes, and food cost money out in the real world.

As if to help speed up the future the C bus he'd been waiting on at the bus stop at Spring Garden Street letting a bunch of people off to go about their business. As the crowd he was standing with trickled onto it one by one, until it was only standing room by the time he paid his fare and got on.

Bracing himself on a tall pole over his head. As the bus headed close to his neighborhood and uncertain'ty past run down houses and walls full of graffiti. Squinting his eyes a little, he recognized a spray pain'ted named "CAT" in bright pain't a brief sadness settled into him at the sight. His homeboy CAT had got killed in the Chow Hall at D.C. in 1995 after only being down for six months.

Continuing to check the scenery as the bus passed, Telly paid particular attention at the young faces crowded on corners thinking how much the players changed, but the game didn't. Remembering a decade ago different faces on those same corners, including his dark-skinned face.

Anticipating the stop that was his, he started to make his way towards an exit. By the time he maneuvered his way through the thick crowd, the bus arrived at his destination: Susquehanna and Dauphin. The neighborhood he was born and raised in, where only the strong survived and the weak crumbled.

Stepping onto the pavement in his prison issued blue shirt and slacks with black TImberland boots on. As the bus drove off behind him. He just stood there for a moment, scanning the landscape. Looking at the Deli on the corner in front of the subway tunnel whereas far back as a decade ago, he ran down on an enemy strapped with a 45 caliber handgun emptying out his whole clip. Leading to the prison bid he'd just came home from.

Feeling no regrets, he began to walk on his way through crowds of people on the corner, past the neighborhood basketball courts and trash filled vacant lost. Past liquor stores and barber shops, until he reached a brown brick, three story apartment building.

Turning the knob to open the wooden door, and finding it locked. He put his fingers around his mouth then screamed in the direction of the highest window. "YO!!!! Tanya!!!!.... Tanya!!!!!"

A few minutes later, the window slid up. Then the woman poked her head out to see who was calling. Looking down she smiled and said, "I'll be right down boo"

Standing at five feet eleven inches, light skinned, with a round medium sized ass, and perky breasts. Tanya was a very beautiful woman from head to toe. Still smiling she raced downstairs to open the front door. Then Immediately on onto the payment wrapping her arms around his waist, while he hugged her in return, appreciative of how pleasurable her body felt against his.

She was his high school sweetheart and baby mama. The only family he had besides his daughter. He had no siblings, and his mother passed away while he was doing his bid. Then his grandmother passed shortly after. His aunts, uncles and cousins weren't shit throughout his whole bid. They never communicated either by phone or visitation. Even the few times he called on the phone, they always seemed in a rush to get rid of him. So as far as he was concerned, didn't none of them exist.

Throughout his decade bid, Tanya was the only one that held him down with the little money she could provide and visits she could make. The inconsistency of her support didn't really matter though because it was the thought that counted. For that reason alone, he would always love her no matter what kind of twists fate brought to their lives.

Turning her lips to meet his, they engaged in a long slow french kiss. Once finished Tanya said, "We better get inside before Tahira kills me. She's been anxious all morning." "Oh, word?"

"Yeah. Actually, she's been anxious ever since I told her you were coming home, which was about a week ago. She's upstairs cooking you something to eat right now. I told her how much you liked fried fish and french fries."

Telly followed Tanya inside and closed the door behind him. After locking the door, astonished, he asked, "She can cook already?"

Climbing up the stairway she said "Yup, she knew how to cook ever since she was nine. I told you how smart she was. She picks up on things real quick."

"She got me beat then. My cooking game is on a zero. But of course, you already know that." Telly said smirking.

Looking back at him and turning down her lips she giggled saying, "Yes I do".

Checking out her short, curly black hair from behind as well as the shape of her ass in the spandex bottoms she wore. While climbing the squeaky wooden stairs that led to her two-bedroom apartment on the third floor. Involuntarily, he felt himself rise at the sight of her ass jiggling as she took the steps in front of him.

Reaching the halfway open black covered door of her apartment. She walked in without breaking her stride. Behind her he followed, closing the door once he was inside. Then he Immediately began to take in the view, quietly concerned about the state of things. Understanding that things were his responsibility now.

At the thought of his family responsibilities. Out of the kitchen doorway came his ten-year-old daughter Tahira wearing some blue colored Nike nylon sweatpants with white Air Force ones, and a white tee, looking a split Image of her mother. She just had Telly's dark colored skin.

"What's up shortie!", Telly said with a smile. "Nothing", she said crossing the space between them, giving him a hug and kiss. Holding her at arm's length, he said "I heard you was in here cooking."

With a look of pride on her face she said, "Yeah, I made you some fish an french fries. Plus, some homemade biscuits." Then giggling, looking at her mother with innocence only a child has she asked, "Are you home to stay Daddy?" Without a hesitation he responded, "Oh Yeah." Then turned and hurried towards the kitchen. Sitting down in a shabby love seat situated in the corner of the living room, Telly let out a heavy sigh asking, "How much this place cost you a month?"

Taking a seat beside him Tanya answered, "Seven Hundred a month plus utilities." Without a look of contempt on his face, he looked around the small living room then back at her face. "Four Hundred for this little shit. I know I've been gone for a decade, but I know shit ain't change that much." "You're right.", Tanya said, "This is high for an apartment this size. It was the only place I could find that was close enough to Tahira's school. It was either this or the projects, and you know how I feel about that shit."

Feeling shame for placing his family in this position, where they had to struggle just to keep their head above water, Telly said sincerely, "I'm sorry." Not knowing what to say. She said nothing, simply because it wasn't okay. So, there was nothing she could say to make it seem that way, nor did she necessarily want to many times over the years. When things got real rough and she felt alone, she tossed all the blame on his head. True love was the only reason she held him down.

In an attempt to express that love without saying something she didn't even mean, but to let him know she understood, she leaned over and kissed him. Breaking the awkward moment, Tahira appeared out of the kitchen announcing, "The food is ready." Upon hearing, Telly stood himself, then pulled Tanya with him and wrapped his arm around her waist and headed towards the kitchen, where they enjoyed their first meal as family.

Drinking down another bottle of codeine infused yellow cough syrup that he just got from J street, Broke stood unnoticed in the dark walkway of an abandoned building. Watching as the hustlers on 20th and York made drug sales, thinking to himself just a little bit longer, then these hustlers, just like the rest would have to pay their taxes or else.

Usually he didn't come out this far, preferring to patrol areas that he was more familiar with, where he actually knew who was getting money. But since he was sexing this girl named Keisha who lived a few blocks away from where he was standing. He couldn't help but notice these guys down here caking off and shining like the sun. So naturally they would have to pay homage. He didn't believe in discrimination.

As the high from the syrup settled in on him, through his eyes suddenly everything seemed to slow down. Giving him the perception that everybody was moving in slow motion. Even himself as he reached for the zipper on the bottom bookbag that was sling across his left shoulder, zipping it halfway open, revealing a grayish colored Mac.

Pulling it out of its concealment with his black gloved hands, leaving the empty bookbag still sling across his shoulder. He jerked back the hammer on the automatic weapon, then stepped out the dark walkway he was observing in towards the corner where the young hustlers stood waiting on customers, trying to stay in their blind side, to insure they didn't see him coming.

Cutting in between two parked cars, he held the Mac low behind his legs then after a car passed down the one-way street, he hurried across to the opposite to the opposite sidewalk. Quick strides taking him up to the corner on which the hustlers stood turning the corner quickly, he aimed the Mac with two hands, "Don't nobody move or they getting wet!"

Freezing in place like a rabbit cornered a make, all five of young men did as they were told seeing in Broke's eyes, that he meant what he said.

"Now lay face down on the ground and keep your hands where I can see them.", he commanded.

Like a slave under a master's whip, they obeyed. Then once they were all face down on the ground, Broke knelt and went from man to man expertly relieving their bodies of all valuables. Jewels, money, drugs, and even two handguns, leaving no proverbial stone unturned, placing everything inside the brown bookbag. Done in less than five minutes, he stood up. Then, as quickly as he came, he left, leaving the young men laying face down on the concrete sidewalk too scared to move a muscle.

For as long as he could remember, he'd always been called Broke. Growing up in a poverty-stricken community amongst the poor, his family was the poorest. Always eating at the soup kitchens, getting clothes from the salvation army, always in a worse state of existence than everybody else. So, in the way of ghetto children universally, the neighborhood kids nicknamed him "Lil Broke". Now he stands over six feet tall, brown skinned, weighing two-hundred and twenty-five pounds. He was no longer little, nor was he necessarily broke.

By the time he was old enough to hold a gun his monetary situation ceased to be a problem. Ironically, Some of the same kids that nicknamed him Broke now contributed to the lifestyle he main'tained. He was a Broadie Boy A.K.A. Stick-Up kid. Plain and simple. The hustlers made money and he took the money. Either the hard way or the easy way. No matter who they were, or what they represented.as far as he was concerned, the hood owed him. And he liked the saying "There is nothing more dangerous than a broke nigga that's focused." He even held his own crew, "The Broadie Boyz".

Sitting with some of his soldiers now, in one of the houses located in North Philly. Broke sat slouched down on a black leather couch, counting the stacks of money he'd just got from 20th and York while methodically drinking down another bottle of yellow syrup, while his soldiers watched him admirably.

They loved him with all their hearts, willing to follow him through hell and back. This was simply because he led by example, still in the trenches, even though he was a top General, So naturally niggas was feeling that.

Scratching his chest from the effects of the syrup, in a slow voice Broke said, "Goddamn. Them niggas up there is getting it." Looking at the seven stacks of money that was lined up on a wooden table situated in front of Broke. Snuff, a captain in the organization asked, "Who?"

"Them niggas up there on 20th Street. I had to run down on 'em. And let them know shit is real. They been under the radar like a muthafucka." said Broke. Pausing to scratch, he looked up from counting. "If I wasn't fucking that chick from around there, I'd never known."

Looking at the ceiling of the sparsely furnished room, thoughtfully after about a minute, Snuff looked back ad Broke, "20th and what?"

"20th and York, right by the bar" said Broke. "Aiight! ASAP. Ima get some grimeys out there to let them know this isn't no one time thing," said Snuff.

Smiling, Broke continued to count the money. Snuff was his favorite captain. Always taking initiative in a situation which was what Broke liked. Still fairly young at the age of twenty-four, Broke figured he'd give homie a little while longer. Then promote him up a notch.

Finished counting now, Broke looked up with raised eyebrows, "Fifty Grand! In they pockets on the corner! Where in the hell do these niggas think they at?" With that being said, the whole room burst out laughing. Then somebody across the room piped in "With them little shits".

Looking at the two black nosed38 handguns, that lay beside the stack of money, the whole room started laughing harder. Broke and his boys didn't use nothing but big guns that ripped through armored vehicles like it was swiss cheese.

Interrupting the laughter, a teenager peeled his head through the front door. "It's somebody out here to see Broke." Glancing in the direction of the teenager, Broke asked, "Who is it." "It's a tall, dark skin dude who say his name is Telly." Staying in deep thought for a few minutes, suddenly a look of surprise came over Broke's face. "Tell him I be right out."

"Aiight." The teenager said closing the door back. Grabbing the stacks of money and placing them in the bookbag with the Mac, while zipping it shut, Broke said, "You'll split the drugs and shines up amongst ya'll selves. I don't need it." As the men moved towards the table to divide it up evenly, Broke headed to the front door with a rave smile on his face.

Telly was standing outside the Broadie Boyz stash house, still dressed down in his prison issued clothes. He had no other clothes to wear. Tell stood with his back turned to the house in silence, watching as the ghetto came alive on this May midmorning. Telly was in his thoughts thinking about the sex marathon that took place between himself and Tanya last night, as well as this morning when they both woke up. Truth be told, he didn't want to stop this morning. It took considerable willpower to climb out of bed from Tanya. Her sex game was contagious like that, leaving him yearning for more. Just like a crack addict craves for crack.

But the pressing matters of his situation prevailed. He needed to get on his feet. Staying in bed and fucking wasn't gonna do that. Besides, he could continue where he left off later on tonight.

Hearing the door to the stash house open behind him, he turned around and looked up the steps. Involuntarily a smile broke on his face. Not just from the fact that he finally found Broke after searching for hours trying to find him, but also because he was truly happy to see his childhood friend.

Walking down the steps towards Telly, Broke extended his hand saying, "Damn nigga you done got big as hell! When you get out?"

Shaking Broke's extended hand, Telly said, "I got out yesterday, and from what I'm hearing when I was down, shit I ain't the only one that done got big. Damn near everybody I ran into swear up and down that you was bigger than life. So, you know I had to get in touch."

Disengaging from their handshake, Broke said "Yeah, you know how it be. Its only right. Life been showing me its ass for a long time." Thinking about how hard Broke had it coming up, Telly nodded his head in agreement. "True dat fam. Life's still showing me its ass." said Telly.

Stepping back, Broke took in Telly's wardrobe for the first time, then turned to one of his soldiers sitting on the steps. "Ayo, go grab that bookbag for me. It's sitting on the table."

The same teenager that got Broke a few minutes ago, jumped up and ran inside. In a flash, he was back, carrying the brown bookbag in one hand while walking down the steps to hand it to Broke. "Good look youngbuck", Broke said taking the bookbag. Then turning towards Telly, he said, "Let's go for a ride". Walking side by side they headed down the sidewalk, until about halfway down, they come to a midnight blue, four door, seven series B.M.W. Broke pulls out a keychain and pressed a button.

Instantly the sound of locks coming open was heard. Then crossing in between parked cars with black dickie suit and black Timberland boots on, Broke headed towards the driver's side saying, "What you waiting on nigga. Get in."

With a look showing that he was clearly Impressed, Telly climbed in the passenger side at the same time Broke was getting in. Once the doors were closed, Broke zipped open the bookbag and placed the Mac on his lap. He then threw the bookbag of money on the floor under the seat. He put the keys in the ignition and turned the key. Immediately, the sounds of the rapper Nas blared from his five thousand dollar stereo. "Who's world is this?...Its Mine, It's Mine, It's Mine....Who's world is this?....It's Yours..." Pulling out of his parking space, Broke patted the Mac 11 on his lap. "Shit is real out here fam". Remembering all the stories he heard from homies inside. Telly responded, " Yeah I heard".

Driving through the ghetto streets of North Philly. For a time, every corner that they passed, niggas was showing love at the sight of Broke's car. Saluting and screaming, "What up" as they come through. Reinforcing in Telly's mind the ghetto celebrity status homies inside said Broke has attained.

Then ad they got farther and farther away from the stash house, the tension in the air from hustlas on corners was palpable. Inside those cold stares could be found the victims of the juggernaut Broke built. These were die hard resisters. The ones who banged out when the Broadie Boyz came collecting.

Refusing to give up willingly what they grinded hard to make. No matter how outnumbered and out-gunned they were, in the end though, the inevitable happened. Leaving their shit splattered and money taken anyway.

Staring back at the hustlas just as hard. Broke asked, "So what's on your mind yo? I know you ain't just came around to say hi." Glancing towards Broke he answered, "I'm fucked up and trying to get on my feet." "Enuff said fam. Do you know what I got going on though?"

"Naw, not exactly. From my understanding though, they say you on some gonna shit. Some black I.R.S. shit." "Yeah, that's basically it. The same shit I been on all my life. Although what's taking place now is on a bigger scale. Organized and everything. With a structure of chain and command similar to the military." Turning his head to look Telly in the eye he asked, "You think you can deal with that?' The look in eyes made Telly hesitate for a split second, then with a nod of his head Telly said, "No doubt".

Fixing his attention back on the road, Broke made a left turn onto Broad Street, driving past several stop lights before speaking another word. "We'll see", he said cryptically. As he reached under the seat inside the bookbag producing a stack of money. "Right now, though, here's some dough to get you up and running. Get some clothes to wear and shit like that. A coming home present from me." Reaching over, Telly took the money from his extended hand. "I appreciate it man." "Ain't shit fam, it's from the heart", he responded, checking his speed ad a blue and white squad car cruised past them in the opposite lane.

They were now near a shopping mall downtown called "The Gallery", where Broke planned to drop Telly off to do some shopping while he went to handle his business for the day. Pulling onto a side street a couple of blocks from the Gallery, Broke drove halfway down the one-way street before coming to a stop. "Aiight yo, enjoy yourself. I got to handle some B.I., but I'll see you tonight. Just come back through the stash house where we just left from. Meet me there at 9:00. And I'll put you down with what's going on."

Stashing the stacks of money in he'd been given in his socks. Simply because he had no pockets on his prison slacks. He extended his hand towards Broke. "Again yo. I appreciate it fam." Nodding his head, Broke shook his hand. Then Telly climbed out the passenger side closing the door behind him. Heading towards the direction of the Gallery mall. While Broke drove the Beemer around the corner and out of sight.

Chapter

3

Checking the authenticity of the dollar bill in the streetlight, the black taxi driver broke out in a big grin. "Thanks brother I appreciate the tip."

"You're welcome yo, trust me, I know how it is", Telly said nodding his head while at the same time hugging the last of the shopping bags out the trunk of the taxi. Closing the trunk and heading towards the driver's door. Before climbing in, the taxi driver yelled towards Telly's back, "Don't forget how that number on the card I gave you is twenty-four hours. If you ever need a ride, don't hesitate to call, no matter what the time." Smiling at the desperation heard in the man's voice, Telly nodded his head to show that he understood, then headed on through the apartment door, paused for a second to shut it behind him. Then climbed the stairwell towards their apartment on the third floor.

As he stepped inside with both hands filled with shopping bags, Tanya asked with one hand on the doorknob, "Is that all of it?" "Yeah", he said placing the bags with all the rest situated on the living room floor. After pushing the door shut, she headed towards the couch excited. Taking a seat in front of the many shopping bags covering the floor. "So, which one is mines?", she asked.

Looking at Tanya sitting on the couch. Then at Tahira standing across the room with a playful look in his eyes Telly said, "Pssst.... which one is yours? I know that's right...Ain't none of them yours. This for me and Tahira."

Smirking, Tanya sat up on the edge of the couch, "Stop playing! Which one is mine?" Suddenly, sounds of laughter erupted from Tahira. While still smirking, Tanya headed towards the bags. "Get out the way. I'll find them myself." Dodging her push, Telly went and sat on the couch watching in satisfaction as Tahira and Tanya started looking through the bags from the different stores. City Blue, Strawbridge's, The Polo Shop, Foot Locker, The Net, etc. Is seemed as though he went everywhere. He had been all over the place looking for things that he knew would please his small family as well as provide him with the clothes he needed, spending money in excess of three thousand dollars.

At first, he planned on just getting a few things while saving the bulk of the money for essential stuff like food, rent, and utilities for the apartment. Then after a moment's thought, he decided to go ahead and splurge realizing how much money he was bound to make if just on a whim Broke just gave him five thousands like that "as a present". Without even pausing to blink or take a breath completely unconcerned with its value. So, he's called home to Tanya who had taken a day off from work asking the sizes of her and Tahira as well as what kind of things really interested his daughter. Finding to his surprise that at age ten and a half she is already into designer clothes and what not. Preoccupied with keeping up with the "Joneses". When at her age when he was young, he could remember his primary concern was having fun. Back then he could care less how he looked.

Looking at Tanya's smile, as she pulled out her clothes. He could tell him so much stuff was unexpected. Yeah, she probably expected a little something but not like this. Nor as expensive as what he got either. In front of her was all the latest casual wear. From Donna Karan to Baby Phat, Air Jordans to Inversons. Being able to provide for his family gave him a natural high shared by father's and husbands everywhere.

Stopping in the middle of going through another bag, Tanya walked over to stand in between his open legs, then bent over and gave him a long slow french kiss. "Thank You" she said, with a sexy smile. When she really wanted to know how he could afford all this stuff. "You like my taste in clothes so far?"

Cupping his balls in his new blue Polo jeans he had on she answered, "Yeah and Ima show you just how much I like it in a little while." Glancing over her shoulder at his daughter, oblivious to everyone except the shopping bags she opened. Telly looked at the time on the circle clock on the wall which showed Eight Thirty P.M. Reluctantly he looked back at Tanya, "That sounds real good but we gonna have to postpone that for later. I got somewhere I need to be at nine." "What time you plan on being back?" "I don't know." Giving him a quick kiss on the lips she said, "Well if I'm asleep, wake me up alright? And be careful. You can use my keys until you get a set made." Closing his legs shut and standing up, Telly headed across the room past a now attentive Tahira, looking at him with a questioning look on her face. "I'll be back in a few hours" he said, muffling her neatly done hair up with his hand. "Daddy!" she said, jerking away knowing what she was going to do. He laughed, amused at her preoccupation with her looks at a young age, thinking to himself while heading out the door that she probably got that from her mother, which was all good. As far as he was concerned, she would have all the luxuries she wanted.

Stepping out into the warm night air, geared down in polo jeans, black short sleeved polo shirt and black quarter length Timberland boots. Telly walked with purposeful strides through the extra crowded sidewalks of people standing around involved in various activities. All year round, the streets stayed full of people. More though when it was warm outside like it was right now.

Many summers when Telly was down, he would have gave everything to be amongst these same people, standing around enjoying their freedom, In whatever suited their formay, whether they were broke winos hanging out on abandoned stoops, or money getting drug dealers getting paid. Freedom in any form was truly something to be cherished. It's a shame though he had to be one of those certain individuals who lost their freedom on a daily basis simply just trying to survive the storm, "none the less". Life was like that for a lot of people, what choice did he really have? He thought to himself, who wanted to have a convicted murderer?

Reaching the block that the stash house was on, he smiled to himself. The answer to his question was right in front of his face. It was people like Broke who hired convicted murderers...In the darkness of the building ahead, Snuff pulled out his 45-caliber pistol just as Telly got closer to where he stood. "What's Up Yo!!", he said in a menacing voice. Looking in Snuff's direction and seeing the silhouette of a gun in Snuff's hand, Telly stopped where he was at saying, "I came to see Broke." Looking Telly up and down checking his description against the information Broke gave him Snuff asked, "What's your name?" "Telly."

Glancing over to the same teenager from that morning who was sitting on the steps when Telly first came through Snuff asked, "This the same dude came through earlier!?" With a nod he gave his verification. Relaxing a little, Snuff kicked his gun away. "My bad yo. You can never be too careful out here." Telly nodded his head. "Yeah, I see, Everybody keep reminding me." "Past two weeks ago, my cousin got slumped the same way, standing in front of his baby mother's house slippin, when some nigga just calmly walked down the block. Then BOOM! That was it. Dead before he hit the ground." "Damn that's fucked up!" Nodding his head in agreement, Snuff stuck out is hand. "They call me Snuff. Nice to meet you. Broke told me a little about you." "Yeah, we ran together from time to time." Walking towards a new black colored Chevy Malibu, Snuff said, "Broke ain't here. He at another spot. He told me to bring you there once you came."

Following behind him, Telly went to the passenger side, while Snuff went around and climbed in the driver's side. "It's open yo", Snuff said, closing the door. Climbing in and shutting the door Telly slouched down in his seat as Snuff started the car. He wondered why Broke would tell him to come here if he knew he wasn't gonna be here. "You smoke treez?", snuff asked while pulling out the parking space. "Yeah". Passing Telly a sandwich bag full of marijuana from out his pocket along with two Philly blunts. He said, "Roll that up then. It's that fire." Going through the procedures needed, Telly concentrated on the task at hand as Snuff navigated through the street of North Philly out towards Lehigh Ave where Broke was waiting on their arrival.

"So, where all you been at? I got a brother that's knocked right now." "Where at? I done been all over mostly. But most of my time was done at Gratersford." "That's where he at! He been down eight joints. His name is Big Lord. Muscle bound nigga, dark skinned, and rock cornrows."

Without having to search his memory, because Big Lord was a popular dude, Telly said, "Yeah, I know that nigga, Used to work out with him sometime. Shit, everybody know that nigga."

"What he be doing?" "Mostly laying back and doing a little grindin. Every now and then he put down a demonstration." Laughing, Snuff said, "Yeah I know how he is. I love that nigga." Putting the finishing touches on the last blunt, Telly handed the sandwich bag to Snuff. Then reached down in the rest where he saw a lighter. Then blazed the blunt, exhaling smoke slowly through his nose. Instantly he found Snuff's words true. The weed he was smoking was indeed fire. Passing the blunt to Snuff, then sparking up the other one. They kept up a steady rotation for the rest of the ride. Not saying anything to each other. Just enjoying the weed filled blunts. Until finally, Snuff came to a stop beside a dark alley. He turned the car off and got out, beckoning for Telly to follow him through.

Walking through the dark trash filled alleyway. Behind what appeared to be abandoned houses with their broken and boarded up windows. Past stray cats and urine filled 40 oz bottles up against the walls. After coming halfway through, Snuff led them towards the back door of one of the abandoned houses. Stepping with sure steps over obstacles in the dark. With the strides of a person completely familiar with his surroundings.

Knocking three times on the raggedy steel door before entering. Snuff walked inside followed by Telly. Into a dark area that appeared to be a burnt kitchen. Then Immediately to their right, upon closing the door, he led the way down a dark stairwell into a concrete basement. Which was illuminated by a solitary propane lantern. Sitting in the middle of the floor showing the shapes of four bodies surrounding a man tied to a metal chair. Binded at ankles, arms, and mouth. The first thing that went through Telly's mind at the sight was the look in Broke's eyes that made him hesitate in the car. Seeing this, now he partially understood. "Thought it was a game huh", Broke said, standing in front of the seated man. "I'm very disappointed in you."

Suddenly Broke's brass knuckled right gloved fist struck out like lightning, landing directly on the left eye of the seated man's already bloody face. Sending a burst of blood squirting from another tear. In the man's heavily bruised light skinned face. Causing the man to grunt through his gag in agony. With his voice steadily rising, Broke said, "I gave birth to you nigga!.... Gave you a style to run with!......Put you in a position of respect!!...Now you turn your back on me?!!...Give me your ass to kiss????!!!!"

Instantly following these words Broke let loose with a barrage of punches from his brass knuckled fist. Hooks, jabs, uppercuts, rained all over the victim's face. Sounds of bones cracking in his face were repeatedly heard. As blood flew in different directions. Not only drenching the victims face. But also, a considerable amount was on the front of Telly's jumpsuit. As well as the Immediate area surrounding the metal chair.

Stopping just as sudden as he started. Breathing heavily Broke looked at his handy work. Watching in pleasure as the mans head hung low. Unconscious from the unbearable pain inflicted. Amazing though still breathing shallow breath. Although it was clear to everyone in the room. That he was merely an inch from death. After taking a such a brutal beating like that. Glancing over towards Telly as if just watching him for the first time. Then at Snuff standing close beside him. Broke pointed to Telly. "Give Telly your gun Snuff." As Snuff handed Telly his

Smith Wesson 45 handgun, Broke punched the victim in the face with a right hook yelling, "Wake up Bitch!"

Gaining consciousness from the blow. The man somehow managed to lift his head partially up. Whereas though he was looking his tormentor in the eye. "You see this nigga right here Telly?"

"Yeah", Telly responded straight faced. "He went against the grain. Spit in my face so to speak. When all I ever did was empower this nigga. Like I do everybody in our family." Pausing for a second, he looked in the man's eyes. Then after a brief moment continued, "See, that's what we are Telly. One big family. And I love all my grimmey's as if we came from the same mother. Can you feel that yo?' Looking at Broke's penetrating stare, Telly nodded his head in agreement. "I mean, can you really understand. What I mean when I say family?" Answering his own question he continued, "I mean bonded forever. Till death do us." Starting to feel like he was in over his head. Hearing the sound of conviction in Broke's voice. Before he could fully analyze exactly what he was feeling Broke said "Slump that nigga yo."

With only a moments hesitation, in spite of the uncomfortable feeling he felt. Telly brought the handgun up in his right hand. Moved around until he was standing directly in the victims eyes. Aimed the gun towards the man's forehead. Then even as the man weakly shook his head in a pleading manner. Telly pulled the trigger of the powerful handgun. Sending fragments of the man's brain and skull spraying out the back of his head. As his body shook uncontrollably in the confines of the metal chair. Standing with ringing ears from the sound of the gun in such an enclosed place. Telly looked in Broke's watchful face of approval. And couldn't help but wonder if the shaking of the man's head was for fear of death, or a silent warning to him.

Sliding the bloody bras knuckles off his equally saturated gloves. Broke looked towards his captains. "Get rid of the body." Then turned back towards Telly. "Welcome aboard fam. Since I already know your gangsta, I'm making you a captain. You'll take over the area that he once commanded.", he said, pointing to the dead body. "Our organizational structure is pretty simple. You got Foot Soldiers, Lieutenants, Captains, and Generals. I'm the highest ranking General naturally. Since this is the house I built from the ground up." Noticing he still held the pistol gripped in his hand. Telly looked towards Snuff came over and took it away. Immediately beginning to take the weapon apart. In preparation of its disposal. Watching him at work Broke said, "Yeah we do that sometimes depending on the situation. We got plenty of hammers. That's why niggas can't stop us.... Anyway though, let me finish explaining shit to you..."

For the next hour, Telly stood there listening attentively, as Broke ran down the organizational structure and what was expected of him as a member of the organization.

Kicking both the front and back door open at the same time. Running in with guns drawn commanding everybody to get to the floor. From the swiftness and expertise of the masked men entering the room. The occupants of the dope house on 60th street. At first thought the intrusion was the work of the police. Then slowly recognition dawned on them. As they lay face down on the floor with hands behind their head. "Ya'll know what it is!!", Telly yelled behind his black ski mask. "I'm only gonna ask one time! Where the stash at?!"

For approximately one minute not a sound was heard. None of the black men laying down under gun point wanted to be the first to give into their demands. Even though everyone of them was scared to death. Each knowing full well the reputation of the notorious "Broadie Boyz".

Suddenly, Telly brought the butt of the Mac 9 he held in his hands down hard on the nearest man. Using all of his strength in his two hundred and forty frame. Breathing the silence of the poorly furnished room. With the sounds of a wooden stock meeting bone. Causing instantly blood to seep out between the victims cornrows. Smashing viciously down again and again. While the man weakly tried to protect himself. Curling his body up into a fetal position. From across the room someone yelled out, "It's some in the basement! And some upstairs!" Leaving the now unconscious form of the victim. Telly navigated the floor towards the man who gave instruction. Then reached down and yanked him to his feet. "Where upstairs?" "In the first bedroom inside the closet. It's a hole inside the wall behind some boxes." Looking over at one of his soldiers standing on the wooden steps. With his gun Telly pointed in the upstairs direction. "Go ahead and grip that up." Then turning his attention back to the man beside him. "Take me downstairs to the other stash." Without having to be told. Telly's lieutenant Petey Immediately got to work. Taking initiative while Telly went down into the basement. Commanding his men to strip everybody down. Taking into possession anything of value. Emerging from the basement about eight minutes later. Holding now in one hand, a completely filled Glad trash bag. Looking around the living room of the dope house. Telly noticed the only man left to search was the one that had taken him the stash.

Pushing the man from behind. Sending him falling face down on the ground. Telly looked towards his soldiers saying, "C'mon y'all, we out. Somebody check this nigga right here though."

Quickly, everybody started to file out. Leaving as quickly as they came. Running outside towards the stolen cars waiting on them. Climbing into their assigned cars with no problems. Then suddenly a gunshot rang out from inside the house. Followed by Petey running out to join them in the car. Climbing in the car that Telly was in. In his hand Petey held a diamond bracelet with blood on it. Curiously, Tell asked, already knowing the answer, "What happened?"

"Nigga tried to tuck the bracelet. So, you know how that go." As the car pulled off, Telly just shook his head. Inwardly amused at how much Petey resembled him when he was younger. Always trying to find a reason to shoot somebody after a robbery.

Chapter

4

A month and a half passed since Telly's membership that night. Since then, he'd been living up to the hype. Putting down several demonstrations to all opposition. Successfully clamping down on the majority of his area. Whereas when he first came aboard. The area he'd been assigned was pretty much virgin. Just really beginning the campaign of locking things down. Counting up the last of the money taken from the dope house. Telly looked over towards Petey sitting across the table. "Seventy-five thousand and five hundred dollars. Plus, two bricks of crack and four hammers."

Nodding his head in satisfaction Petey said, "I know just the right nigga to take those off your hands too. He stay up my grandma way. Near Saigon Projects from 13th in South Philly." "How much you think you can get for it?' "Shit, about at least thirty and some change. And that's including the hammers. Trust me fam. What them nigga's is paying for work out there now. Two birds for thirty, plus hammers. It's a discount like a muthafucka.'

Pushing the guns and two bricks of cocaine over towards Petey. Telly reached down beside him and grabbed up a blue colored gym bag. Then started to pack the money inside. In preparation to be delivered to his superior. Still in awe after a month and half on the job. At how much money the organization made on a daily basis. From spots ranging from North Philly to West. So much money circulated amongst the organization. That on top of members getting paid on a weekly basis. Anything taken besides money was theirs to do with as the captain pleased. And with the utmost pleasure members from different spots took complete advantage. Not just taking drugs and jewelry. They also confiscated drug dealers cars at will. Taking them some whips to the chop shop to get plated up and repain'ted. Then pushing some whips all around Philly. Sunk down in driver seats like it was theirs originally.

The kind of organization the Broadie Boyz were, was not a drug gang. Which was what he initially though. Thinking from the things he heard that they were like the JBM (Junior Black Mafia) in the eighties. Instead, though he'd come to find out as a whole, they just exclusively took money. By laying claim to territories just like the government. Then demanding those people to pay them in order to continue business. Or get hunted down by their many shooters.

The only money that was made came from various money laundering activities. In which Broke chose to invest the bulk of the money towards legitimate businesses—Barbershops, Beauty Salons, Night Clubs, Cafes, Bars, Real Estate, etc. All being run by top Generals in the organization. Who had proven their loyalty and competence time again.

Zipping the gym bag shut after placing the last stack inside. Telly stood saying, "Aiight lil homies that's a wrap for the day. I'll see you tomorrow fam." Aiight", Petey responded nodding his head. Grabbing hi 40 caliber pistol and placing it in his wristband. Telly slung the money filled gym bag across his shoulders. Then walked from out the kitchen towards one of the low key cars that was kept for them so they could get around without brining too much attention.

Making it outside where soldiers sat lounging on the steps. Telly walked around them and to a car parked by the curb. Climbed inside and shut the door. Then pulled off just as the streetlights came on. Navigating the black colored Monte Carlo through the crowded West Philly streets. Headed to meet his superior at one of the Broadie Boyz Bars. In order to drop off the day's take. The same way he did several days out the week.

Lighting up a blunt he'd rolled earlier. As he inhaled the sweet smoke. He glanced over to the gym bag on the passenger seat. Thinking about the guy that had this job before him. Finding himself still wondering about that night over a month ago. When the man that was strapped in the chair shook his head as if in warning. Right before Telly blew his brains all over the floor. Was it really a warning? Or just the plea of a man facing death…So far, he'd seen nothing to worry about. Still though, he remained on point. If not because of the dead man, then because of the vibe he got from Broke in the beginning.

Stopping the car three quarters down a two-way street. Right underneath the El train tracks above the street on 46th. He backed the car into a parking spot. Right across the street from the bar he was going to. Turned off the motor, then sat for a few minutes. Finishing off the blunt he was smoking. Then once done he grabbed up the gym bag. Got up out the car and headed in the direction of the bar.

Coming onto the pavement in front of the neon lights flashing in the bars tinted windows. The sign read "Lacey's Lounge Bar" in green letters. Off to the right side, sitting on the ground, holding a small bottle in a brown bag sat a neighborhood wino. "Say youngblood, can you spare some change?', the wino called out as Telly got closer to the door. Not knowing when he could be down on his luck again. Telly fished in his pocket and pulling out a bill fold. Peeled a twenty off and handed it to the man. "There you go pop. That's enough right there to hold you down for a minute."

Looking at the twenty-dollar bill. The wino's eyes got big as he dramatically said, "Something good is gonna happen to you." Putting his billfold away Telly Laughed. As he headed on Inside Lacey's Lounge. Stopping briefly in the doorway. In order to let his eyes, adjust to the dimness. All around the room booths and chairs were full as usual. With patrons conversating and ordering drinks from barmaids. While sounds from soul singers of the seventies played softly from speakers. That were strategically placed for maximum effect.

Strolling past the bartender nodding in greeting. Telly walked towards the section off limits to patrons. A stairwell that led upstairs to where his superior was. With a nod the three men that guarded it gave him the okay to go on up. So, without stopping he went on up the stairs. Taking the steps two at a time between his long legs. The room he reached at the top was in complete contrast to the room downstairs. Instead of bare wooden floors, this room had cream plush wall to wall carpeting. Soft expensive leather sofas furnished the room/ As well as glass tables in between couches. Ceiling to floor mirror covered the whole upstairs entirely. And far in the back sipping champagne from a crystal glass, sat Telly's supervisor in a state a relaxation. A one-star General named Lacey.

Crossing the length of the room to where Lacey sat in the darkness in the back Telly spoke in greeting, "What's going on Lacey?" In a rough sounding voice, Lacey responded, "Ain't shit fam. You know the case; I be on a paper chase. How things with you?"

"Every day free is a good day", Telly said, taking a seat. "I can feel that 100%. You want a drink?" "Yeah, let me get some of that corn liquor you keep here." Grabbing the phone beside him, Lacey punched a number then spoke, "Send up a jug of that corn and some glasses to go with it." Hanging it up he looked towards Telly all business. "So, what's the take for today?"

"Seventy-five grand and five hundred.", he responded passing over the gym bag. "We got that from one of Tone's dope spots. Tone was a drug dealer who refused to be extorted. Looking at the gym bag, Lacey smiled. "He gonna be a mad muthafucka tonight. You heard any about his whereabouts?"

"Naw nothing. Some of the lil homies shot up one of his top dawgs though. Nigga in I.C.U." "Pride is a dangerous thing yo. I can't understand it sometimes."

Coming from out the stairwell holding a gallon of corn liquor and glasses. A beautiful dark skin woman walked towards them. Placing it all on a glass table separating Lacey and Telly.

Reaching for the jug and glass to pour a drink Telly said, "Thanks." "Your Welcome", she said with a big smile. Then turned to go back downstairs.

"Let me ask you a question Telly", Lacey said thoughtfully. "If you was faced with some niggas like us, would you pay out or hold it down?"

Drinking down the corn liquor enjoying the burn in his chest, Telly answered, "Pay out. No doubt. What choice would I really have?" "Exactly man. That's why I say I don't understand it. Pride cometh before the fall." Leaning back, Telly gulped down some more liquor. Nodding in agreement at the truth of his words.

Chapter

5

Bobbing her corn-rowed head up and down slowly. The woman sucking on his dick savored every moment. Turning her head from side to side lovingly. As if she were french kissing. Trying to give her lover as much pleasure as possible before he climaxed on her tongue. Lying on his back on the king-sized bed. Draped in tan colored satin sheets. Broke savored every moment as well. Thinking there was nothing better than for a man to get his dick sucked in the morning. Right when he just woke up from sleeping. After being the recipient of a lot of the same last night.

As the woman's soft lips tightened around the head of his penis, Broke couldn't hold out any longer. Suddenly exploding inside the woman's mouth. Curling his toes as she ran her tongue back and forth across the hole in his penis while he climaxed. After swallowing every drop, she looked at him smiling. "You taste good", she mumbled. "You a freaky bitch", he said playfully. Hopping out the bed towards the bathroom. It was time for him to get started on his busy day. Running the seven-year-old organization he built. So, he headed into the bathroom. In order to wash off the dried sweat that accumulate on his body from last nights sex romp. With a girl he took home from one of the nightclubs last night.

By the time he was fully dressed, the woman he brought back form the club last night had already left the penthouse suite of the Adam's Mark Hotel he occupied. Leaving him alone with his two number one shooters, who sat in the spacious living room drinking cups of coffee, waiting on their boss to make his next move.

In the last couple of weeks, things had gotten real hectic for Broke. On three different occasions in this short period. An adversary named Tone had attempted hits on his life. Leading to shoot outs in different areas. So just to be on the safe side simply because he knew he didn't have eyes in the back of his head. Broke took two of the most notorious killers in his organization. And kept them around him constantly. Figuring in his wisdom that six eyes were better than two. Joining the two in the front room He sat down and poured himself a cup of coffee. "Everything ready to go?", he asked. Animal—a three-star General answered, "Yeah, I called down to the front desk last night, letting them know we need a limo by eight this morning. They said they'd call up when it arrived." Taking a quick sip of his drink, Broke looked at his Movado watch. "We got about fifteen minutes. In the meantime, what have ya'll found out about this muthafucka from West Philly who keep taking shots at me?" "Nothing too much about him. But we found out about his family. We got soldiers laying on his ass as we speak."

Sitting up on the edge of his seat Broke yelled, "What is this nigga a ghost?!!! He seem to know every fucking move I make!!" Speaking for the first time Hakeem—a three-star General said, "We'll find this nigga. It's just a matter of time." "Well in that matter of time. This is what I want done." Pausing, Broke took a sip from his cup. "Kidnap his loved ones. I bet you that will bring this nigga to hell."

Suddenly beside Broke the telephone rang. Picking up after the first ring Broke said, "Yeah". After a couple of seconds, he hung it back up saying "I'll be right down." Looking towards his shooters he said, "It's time to go." After gulping down the rest of his coffee. Broke checked his pockets for his two-way airline tickets. Then left up out the room followed by his shooters. Down the hallway onto the elevator feeling naked because he didn't have his gun with him, being as though he was about to catch a flight.

Two guns were quite sufficient though. Especially in the hands of Hakeem and Animal. Stepping out the elevator into the hotel lobby. Directly outside was parked a white limousine with black tinted windows. Seeing them coming the chauffeur opened the door in anticipation. As they crossed the lobby towards him outside.

"Good Morning Sir.", the chauffeur greeted. Nodding his head in return Broke stopped just short of getting in while facing his shooters. "Aiight ya'll. Hold it down, I'll be back tomorrow night."

Then he climbed inside the limo. Patiently waiting as the chauffeur closed the door behind him. Then headed up front to drive him to Philadelphia International Airport.

Walking through the terminal of R.D.U. in Raleigh, N.C. To Broke, it seemed like he was on another planet. The contrast between down south and up North was legendary. Almost everything was different between the two. The styles of clothing people wore, the way they talked, physical make-up of the women, the mentality. You name it and you could definitely find a distinctive difference.

He was used to it by now though. Especially concerning the women. When he was young, he used to come down south every summer. In order to spend time with his uncle. Away from the hustle and bustle of city life. Experience things he never would have. Coming outside the terminal. Yellow and black taxi cabs lined the airport parking lot. Walking over to a cabbie directly parked in front of the sliding doors. Broke leaned in the passenger side window asking, "Can you take me to Lumberton?" "Gonna have to pay up front though. And it's not cheap. Otherwise, it sounds fine to me.'" He said heading towards the driver's side. Getting in on the passenger side, Broke gave the driver three hundred dollar bills out his pocket. "Will that do?"

Nodding his head, the driver took the bills. In no time they were off on the highway, engaging in small talk on their way.

Glancing over towards Broke the driver asked, "So where you come from? If you don't mind me asking. I got some family members up north." "How you know I was from up north?" "I been a taxi driver for over fifteen years. I can tell the difference easily." "I'm from Philly, You ever been up there?" "Naw, but I been to Jersey though. That's where some of my family lives. In any case, it's all too fast for me. I'm just a good ol' country boy, who likes things slow." "Yeah, I can feel that sometimes. It's nice to get away sometimes. I'm a city boy at heart though." Not really wanting to be talking, Broke left the small conversation at that. So as not to encourage the man anymore. Knowing how familiar and friendly southerners were. Prying into another person's business at will. In total contrast to the standoffish nature of people from the north. Who by right, kept their noses out of other people's business.

In about two hours' time, they reached the city limits of Lumberton. From there Broke directed the taxi driver. Out into the country to a two story house he kept. Then hopped out heading towards the front of his home. Pulling out a key he had stashed in concealment. Then entering inside through his one car garage into a home cloaked in silence. Everything just the way he left it on his last visit.

Closing the door behind him. He crossed the brown carpeted floor to open the blinds. Letting the sun shine into a room that was dark for months. Walked into the kitchen to get a 40 oz of Red Bull. Then seated himself in a living room recliner and picked up the phone. Dialing a number he knew by heart, he waited for a connection. "Ayo Jay. What up? It's me, Broke." "What's up yo?" I just got off the phone and I'm about ready to come and see you."

"Aiight. How long you think you'll be?" "Give me about three hours. Ima bust a grub right quick. Then Ima head out to see you."

"See you then. I got some new shit for you too." "1luv" "One", Jay said hanging up.

Finishing off another 40 oz of beer. Broke steered his Range Rover down a bumpy dirt road. Out in the deep country of Red Springs. Where a person could drive for many miles seeing nothing but wilderness. Without even seeing a streetlight. Or even passing another car on the road.

Throwing the empty bottle out the window into the woods. Broke cut a right down another dirt road. Until he came to a house surrounded by acres of land. See his late uncle's military buddy Jay. Sitting on the porch of his wooden home in army fatigues. Obviously waiting on Broke to arrive.

In the distance a pack of twelve big, black coated Rottweilers stood staring at the approaching vehicle on the side of the home. Looking on the intruder as if ready to pounce. The moment the driver climbed out of the door. In fact, about three started moving towards it. Until Jay called them off with a sound from his lips. Sending the aggressive three back beside the rest. Alert for a command from their master.

Stopping the S.U.V. and turning it off. Leaving the keys dangling in the ignition. Broke hopped out, leaving the door open. Playfully going into a military salute, "General Broke reporting for duty sir." Standing up with a smile on his face Jay said, "cut that shit out!" Laughing, Broke walked over, embracing the older man. Jay was Broke's late uncles, best friend. Having served two tours of duty as an Army man in Vietnam. He was an expert when it came to weapons. Even though he was a little shell-shocked.

Leading Broke around to a big shed that stood off in the distance. Jay opened one of the two huge wooden doors. Revealing inside wooden crates stacked all around the walls. Draped over with canvas to keep the dust out. Preventing it from harming its precious contents.

Pulling open a crate top, Jay reached inside and pulled out a black colored assault rifle with a brown handle. "This right here is an AKM. The new joints I was telling you about. It's the successor to the AK-47. Holds fifty rounds in the magazine."

Reaching out to take it from Jay. Broke analyzed the shape of the weapon. "Kinda look like the original AK. Being as though it don't got a stock." "Better than an AK47 if you ask me", Jay said heading over to another crate.

Reaching inside the crate he pulled out a box of ammo. Handing it over to Broke so he could load the magazine. In a couple of minutes, Broke had it loaded. Then they both walked around towards the back of the shed. Where there was dummies with targets on them situated on trees. In the midst of numerous spent shell casings on the ground.

Cocking the hammer back, Broke aimed at the dummy. Then let loose about twenty-five rounds with the weapon of semi-auto. Before flicking the selector switch setting the rifle on fully auto. Sending a burst of twenty-five rounds at the dummy.

Smiling Jay asked, "You like it?" Looking at the remains of the dummy on the tree, Broke responded, "I love it. How much you want for them? "Two-hundred a rifle. They all brand new because I just got them at a gun show." "Let me get a hundred of them." "I only got forty of them now. But sixty more wouldn't be a problem. I'd have that for you by next week at the least. The week after that at the most." "That's all good then. I'll send the usual women down to pick up as soon as possible.", Broke said, reloading up the empty magazine. "Boy I tell you Jay. O don't know what I'd do without you." "Yeah, yeah, heard it all before." "Naw really fam, I mean it. You got some more AR15's?"

Pausing for a second to check his memory, Jay pulled out a cigarette from his pocket and lighted up. "Yeah I got about ten of those left. I don't see why you like that gun so much. It ain't nothing but the civilian version of a M-16. You might as well get the real thing."

"Shit the way my uncle used to talk about them guns. Ain't no way in hell. He told me them shits got to be babied to run right."

Thinking about his towns in Vietnam. When his military issued M16 would jam up on him if it wasn't squeaky clean. So much that he took to using a AK47 he'd got off a dead Vietcong most of the time. Jay said, "Yeah its some truth to that. But it's still a good rifle. You just got to take care of it like anything else." "I'll pass. Same price like before for the AR15?"

"Yeah" "The money is in the glove compartment of the Range", Broke said, completely trusting.

As Jay walked off in the direction of the S.U.V., Broke again, aimed the AKM at the target. Then with the weapon still on fully auto. He let loose a burst of fifty rounds in an arc. Emptying out the magazine in seconds. Tearing the target dummy into nothing but shreds. Broke smiled.

Chapter 6

Munching off a leg out of a bucket of K.F.C. spicy chicken. Tone spoke through the telephone in between bites. "Why you always trying to play me Tasha?"

Tasha—his baby mother, screamed in answer, "I'm not fucking trying to play you! I didn't make this baby by myself!" "Why the fuck is you screaming. You think I cant hear or something?" Calming down a little she said, I was screaming because you make me so mad sometimes. I need this money to pay your son's HMO bill. Without insurance, most hospitals wont even see him. The ones that do gonna charge crazy money. Knowing she was lying he said, "I thought you paid down on that bill two weeks ago." "I ain't never say no shit like that." "You did and you know you did. That's how come I sent around five hundred by Lisa."

Caught up in her lie she resorted back to her usual tactics. "You a fucking piece of shit Tone! You know I ain't say nothing like that! All the money you fucking making selling that shit and you can't even take care of your son!"

Any mention that he didn't take care of his pride and joy. Always made him mad even though it was no truth to the statement. "Bitch I take real good care of Tyson! He don't want or need for nothing. I know that and you know that, and everybody know that! Your lazy ass just want me to take care of you too. All them niggas you fucking. You mean to tell me they don't give you no dough."

"Fuck you muthafucka! Ima take your ass to court!" She used the same threat every time. Knowing how he felt about being in the spotlight. Where he would have a bunch of people in the government scrutinize his livelihood. Didn't no illegal hustler want that, so every time he folded under her pressure.

"I knew I shouldn't of fucked with you all them years ago. You gave the pussy up too easy. If I knew what I know now, I swear to

God I wouldn't have never fucked you", he said throwing a chicken bon into a bag. "How much you need, you broke bitch." The insults he slung didn't even faze her. She had what she wanted now. "Six-hundred dollars." "I'll send somebody around", he said, slamming the phone down. Starting in on another piece of chicken from out the bucket. He was starting to feel like "free money." Getting extorted by his baby mother on the regular. With threats of taking him to court for child support. Then on top of that the Broadie Boyz was trying to extort him. Out of drug money made from spots in "their area". Robbing his workers at will when he refused. Ultimately costing him more money in the end.

No matter how much money it was they took. He was determined not to pay them niggas a red dime. He might as well start wearing a skirt if he did. He'd been getting money in these spots in West Philly. All the way back before the Broadie Boyz even existed. How did they figure he owed them something! Fuck that! He had some shooters on his team too. Not with endless kind of gunpowder the Broadie Boyz had. But still quite capable. On three different occasions he'd already gotten real close to murdering Broke.

Polishing off another piece of chicken. Throwing the remaining bone into a bag. He reached for the telephone and dialed a number. After several rings a sleepy voice answered, "Hello."

"Lisa what up shortie? You still sleep?" She was a woman he'd known for years and completely trusted. Stashing drugs and money at the house to watch. She was one of a few he had making moves for him. Since he was laying low from the Broadie Boyz. "Yeah, What's up with you?", she said recognizing the voice. "I need you to take six-hundred dollars around to that bitch Tasha." "Some more money?"

"Yeah, ain't no rush though. Whenever you get up. Just take it around to her." "Aiight."

"Ima holla", he said, hanging up. Eating up a hand full of french fries. He shook his head in shame. "Free Money."

Orders had come down the line and decisions had been made. Even though he didn't like it. Telly listened to his superior Lacey attentively. And now was carrying out his orders.

Directing the driver of the stolen Dodge Caravan to pull over. As the driver did what he was told. Telly turned towards his soldiers. "Aiight check this out, Ya'll two gonna get out here and walk up near to the school. Then once they let out, look for the little nigga, After you spot him, follow him. Then as soon as we pull up alongside ya'll. Snatch him and bring him into the van. Be as quick as possible. You understand?

Both of them shook their heads in unison. As Telly slid the caravan door open to let them out. Feeling bad about plotting to kidnap a little kid. That was just a little younger than Tahira. How would he feel if somebody kidnapped Tahira? He shuddered to think of it.

Closing the door behind them. He sat back taking in the scenery. There were in Wynnefield, a middle-class neighborhood in west philly. Near an elementary school named Samuel Gompers. All around then were big houses with lawns in front. Carefully manicured with sprinklers watering the grass. Underneath the hot June sun beaming down through trees. Pain'ting a pretty picture for the casual observer.

After about fifteen minutes had passed. You could hear the ringing of the bell inside the school. Signaling for the dismissal of class. Letting all the children know that school was dismissed for the day. Sending shortly afterwards a swarm of children out its doors. Towards parent's cars waiting for them. Or older siblings come to walk their younger family member's home. Creating the perfect opportunity for people to blend in who didn't belong. Like the two soldiers standing by a mailbox. Looking for Tone's son whom they'd identified earlier that morning. When his mother dropped him off to school. One of the last children to leave the building. Tone's son Tyson came walking down the path right towards them. They let him pass up to a couple of feet.

Then they started to follow him at a causal pace. All the way until they got to where less people were. Suddenly the red caravan Telly was in pulled up beside them. Silently sliding the door back on its hinges. At that moment the two soldiers snatched the nine-year-old boy up off the ground. Holding him in between them by the arms. Rushing on up inside the waiting van. As it rolled off down the street. Leaving no bystanders, the wiser because of the swiftness in the way it happened.

Creeping in his souped up hooptie Pontiac 6000. Tone drove up in the one way in and one way out projects called East Falls. In order rendezvous with one of his workers. Secure in its isolation from enemies. Knowing that the Broadie Boyz had limits too and this cut was one of them. Being small enough for any outsiders to stand out. Parking his car in the back parking lot. Tone jumped out and walked towards a small crap game taking place. The worker he'd come to see was busy rolling dice. Walking backwards out the small crowd. Shaking the dice up in his left-hand Lil B spoke, "When I first started hustlin, the only thing I could move was little try rocks." Then suddenly he let the dice fly screaming, "I used to sell treys!" When the dice hit the wall. Miraculously a set of three's stared the crowd in the face. Bending down, he scooped up his money declaring, "The dice don't lie."

Squeezing his five feet nine inch, slim, light-skinned frame in between the crowd. Tone made his way up front. Then pulling out a rubber band wrapped stack of money. He dropped down two-hundred-dollar bills. Looking over at Lil B saying, "Bet that on your door blow."

Smiling, Lil B matched his bet as well as everyone else's. Then slung the dice against the wall. Instantly it landed on seven to everyone's amazement. Then, leaving the money he won on the ground, Lil B declared to everybody, "Same bet." When all the bets was securely on the ground. He shook the dice up again. Then sling them against the wall. Again, a seven came out instantly. "Hold the fuck up!", Tone yelled as he bent down to examine the dice. "Ain't nothing wrong with them dice. Them shits ain't even mine. These niggas was gambling before I came up here.", Lil B said while scooping all his money in one pile on the ground.

Scraping the green dice on the ground to mark it up. Tone said, "Yeah that'll do it". Then dropped the whole stack of money he held on the ground. "Bet shit on your next point."

Smirking Lil B asked, "How much is that right there?" "Don't worry about it nigga. If you hit, its yours." Pointing to a pile of money that belonged to Lil B he added, "If you don't. that's mine."

Grinning from ear to ear. Lil B rolled the dice with no hesitation. When the dice hit the wall it showed a ten. One of the hardest numbers to hit on the dice. Simply because it was only two ways to hit that number. In the background other men made bets.

Patiently waiting for all bets to be made. Once he was satisfied Lil B trolled the dice screaming, "Big Ben!" The number that showed was an eight. Picking them up again he shook them for effect. Then let them go again. When they stopped rolling the dice. He still didn't crap out, but the number showing was number five. "Scared now ain't you.", Tone joked. "Shit, I know that's right." "Five deuce, cut em loose!", somebody yelled from the crowd.

In response to the statement another person encouraged, "Hit that shit my nigga."

Nodding his head in support. He threw the dice hard against the wall. As they spun around, he said, "Daylight.... Daylight.... come now." When the dice finally stopped spinning it showed seven bringing his streak to a stop also. "Goddamn!", he yelled.

Scooping up the money laying on the ground, Tone joked, "God ain't do it homie." At that remark a trickle of laughter broke out around the crowd. With most of them happy for that crap out. Because until that there, Lil B was killing them. Hitting number after number like it was nothing. Creating the small crowd that it was now. By sending a bunch of people home broke as hell.

As another man picked up the dice. After getting all his money off the ground. Tone motioned for Lil B to follow him out to the Pontiac 6000. Where they could talk business without anyone over hearing. Sitting down on the trunk of the car. Tone handed half of the money won back to Lil B. Knowing he needed it more than him. "Here nigga, I don't need that shit. I was just having fun." Taking the money Lil B said, "Good look fam."

"Ain't shit, don't worry about. So what's the news?" "Same old shit. Just—"

Interrupting their conversation Tone's cellular phone rang out. Pulling it from out his pocket he answered it. "Hello. Who this?"

"Tasha" "Bitch what the fuck you want. I know you got the dough I sent."

"Shut the fuck up! You stupid muthafucka! Its about Tyson", she said, starting to cry.

Hearing her cry filled him with concern. "What's up yo? What about Tyson?"

Through continuous sobs she managed to get out. "They fucking took him. I hate you nigga. Getting my baby caught up in your shit." "What you mean they took him?" "Some guy called the house saying he had Tyson. In the background I heard Tyson's voice too."

Jumping down from off the trunk Tone yelled, "What? Who??"

Crying real hard again she answered, "They-said-you-know-who. And the only way we was gonna get him back alive was if you hand deliver unarmed a hundred grand that you owe them. I-hate-you-muthafucka!!"

Immediately he knew who sent message. He also knew they didn't give a fuck about the hundred grand. What they wanted was his life. And when it came to his pride and joy, he would willingly give it up, but not without a fight. "Where they say meet them?"

"Out in Huntingdon Park at ten o' clock", she whined. "They said come alone or they gonna kill him." Listening to her cry on the other end. He tried to reassure her by saying, "Stop crying yo. I'll get him back. Trust me." He hung up the phone. Seeing the look on his face Lil B asked, "What's up yo?"

"Them Broadie Boyz done kidnapped my son. Saying they wont give him back unless I come personally." In an angry tone Lil B said, "That's some fuck shit yo. Them niggas act like you really owe then something. In all actuality they just greedy. That's some foul shit. Fucking with kids."

"I know, I know", he said in a defeated tone." I'm going out in a blaze though yo."

With that said, he started to dial a number on his phone. Preparing a plan for his fateful meeting.

The few remaining streetlights that hadn't been shot out illuminated Huntingdon in different sections. Shinning down on grass filled with bald spots. From being trodden on by people so many times. The rest of the park stayed cloaked in shadows. Embracing the sinister activities that sometimes take place here. Leaving the participants secure in whatever criminal element they practiced. Upstanding citizens of North Philly knew to avoid this place come nightfall.

Standing in the shadows Telly looked at his watch. It was fifteen minutes until ten. And himself as well as members from their organization. Were kind of tense in anticipation of what was planned. Not knowing what kind of surprise Tone had in store. Hoping he kept true to the code of the streets. By not getting the police involved.

"Man, I hope this nigga ain't call five-o", Petey said out loud voicing everyone's thoughts.

Standing a little ways from him Telly said, "Naw, I doubt it. After all the work we done put in on his operations. If he ain't call the police then, he ain't gonna call them now. I don't think he coming alone though." "Shit, I don't know fam. We done switched the whole game up. We got his shortie." "I still say naw. But I'm on point though. You can trust that. If five-o show up. They gonna run they ass back out of here. When I let my shut ring off", Telly explained patting the Mac-90 he had strapped to his shoulder.

In the distance at on of the entrance's into the park. Some car headlights appeared coming inside. Instantly every Broadie Boy posted inside eyeballed the car. Fingers and triggers, ready to open fire, at the slightest provocation. Until when he got up close in their eyesight. They saw that us wasn't nothing but two older people. Instantly everybody relaxed.

Telly glanced down at his watch again. It was now five minutes until the designated time. "Where the fuck this nigga at?", he questioned. "He gonna be here on time. You can trust that.", Hakeem answered from farther back in the shadows by a bush. "Broke a vicious nigga yo, but smart. I wish I'd thought of this shit. We get to make a little money. Plus slump this nigga."

If looks could kill, Hakeem would have been dead. Off to the side of him stood Animal staring. He wished Hakeem would shut the fuck up about the money. Broke ain't say shit about no money. He just wanted Tone dead. The money part of the equation was Hakeem's idea. Which Animal didn't want no part of, but wasn't gonna hate on his friend. Now this nigga was talking about the money like it was legit. Giving off the Impression that it was sanctioned, involving him.

"Here come another car!", yelled Petey. Concentrating on the situation at hand. Animal squinted his eyes in the headlights direction. "That's definitely his car. I can tell by the fucked up pain't job. He drive that Pontiac to make runs and shit. I don't see who driving past the headlights though."

As it got more into the park Petey said, "It's him." The made a bird call over to one of the soldiers hidden across from them. Immediately two masked men ran out with SKS Simonov rifles drawn. Placing themselves directly in front of the brown Pontiac 6000. Pointing their weapons at the driver. When he came to a stop about ten feet from where they stood. One of the men yelled, "Turn that shit off nigga! And get the fuck out the car! Hurry up!"

Doing as he was told, Tone killed the engine and turned off the lights. Hopping out, he closed the door behind him. "Where my son at?", he asked with no fear. Running up beside him. One man stood pointing his SKS rifle at Tone. While the other took a quick peek inside the car. In order to check to make sure wasn't nobody hiding. Then shoved Tone against the front hood hard. Simultaneously patting his body searching for a gun. "Where the fuck my son?", Tone yelled.

Swinging a left hook with this gloved hand. Hitting Tone in his right eye. The gun man that was checking said, "Shut the fuck up nigga!" Coming from out where he stood in the shadows, Hakeem walked towards the car with a SKS over his shoulder. "Don't worry about your son Tone. We don't want him. It's you we want. And now since we have you. We'll let him go. Now where is the money?" Seeing who was walking towards him. Inside, Tone's spirit rose a little. Recognizing that this was one of the shooters assigned to guard Broke. Glanced past him towards the shadows. Tone hoped Broke was back there somewhere. "How I know that?", Tone inquired. Not wanting to squander the opportunity of getting the money. Hakeem pulled out a cellphone and dialed a number. "Yeah, it's me. Let the little nigga go." Hanging it up, he looked to Tone. "There you go. And that's all the assurance you gonna get too. Trust me when I tell you. I've no purpose in killing your son."

Knowing he didn't have no choice but to believe he said, "The money's in the trunk." Then he started walking towards the trunk. Followed by the gun man still pointing their guns. Hakeem walking beside him. As they all gathered around him at the trunk. Tone placed the key inside the trunk. Then turned and lifted up the hood, falling back towards the ground at the same time. Instantly, the three men surrounding him bodies started to dance from the shells of his two shooters who were laying down inside the trunk. The involuntary pulls of the dying men triggers found nothing but air, while they fell to the ground lifeless. This allowed Tone to quickly get up and grab his UZI with two banana clips. Joined by his shooters now on the street.

What had just taken place happened so fast that it took the remaining three men a few seconds to respond. When they did though it was fierce. With bullets ripping through the old model car. Sending Tone and his men ducking for cover on the other side. Returning fire as they backpedaled towards cover. Out the way of the rain of bullets headed their way.

The safety they felt covered behind the bulk of the old car. Was only a temporary thing for a few seconds. Until the hollow points found their way through the car. Then into the bodies of two of the three. Tone being one of the wounded. Still low and returning fire through. Trying his best to hit Broke. Just knowing he was over in the shadows. While simultaneously looking for an escape route because he was bleeding bad. Dripping blood all over the weapon he held making it slippery to hold.

Apparently one of his shooters had the same idea he held. Jumping up and trying to make a run for the shadows. He was cut down as soon as he left the cover. Giving Tone a chance to quickly make a run. Keeping the car in between him and the men growing for him. Leaving the last man shooting at the Braodie Boyz conservatively now. Knowing he was close to running out of shells.

Coming from out of his cover. Telly ran off to the side a little. Then headed towards the spot he saw Tone disappear in the darkness. Swinging his weapon in a arc taking out the last man. Never breaking his stride as he ran down on Tone. Listening to the path he beat through the bush. Trying to stay parallel to him and not directly behind him. Police sirens could now be heard in the distance.

Loosing blood heavily, Tone slowed his pace. Extremely happy when he heard the sirens. Ready to welcome help, even from the police. Stopping to a standstill out of breath. He figured he'd just wait in the shadow by a park bench until the police made it. Suddenly out of the dark a hail of bullets found his body. Drenching the grass where he stood in his blood. Sending him falling to the ground not knowing what hit him, dead. Moving in to confirm his kill, Telly shot Tone's lifeless body for good measure. Then took off running back where everybody else was at. As the sounds of the police sirens got closer. "Come on nigga! Hurry up!", Petey yelled out the passenger side of a black Cherokee Jeep. Bursting out from the darkness into the streetlight. Telly sprinted to the back right door. Hopping in, as Animal hit the gas, even before he could close the door.

Chapter 7

A full day after Tone was handled out in Huntingdon Park. At eight o'clock pm Broke's flight from down south touched down to a rainy Philadelphia Airport. Greeted by Animal, minus Hakeem. Waiting for him outside the terminal. In a black colored Suburban Truck with light tints on the windows. Putting him down on everything that took place.

Reaching in the glove compartment to grab a .45 handgun out. That he told Animal to bring along so he could arm himself. He leaded back in the soft leather seat. Going over his next plans in his heads. While staring through the window wipers in front. As Animal navigated through the quickest routes he knew towards the urban part of Philly. Picking up the cell phone placed between them. Broke dialed a number, then listened as it rang.

"Yo", a voice answered on the other end. "Lacey what up yo?", Broke greeted.

"Ain't shit fam. Holding down the fort that's all", he responded recognizing the voice.

"Check this out. Round up Telly and Petey at the lounge for me. Me and Animal on our way there now."

"Aiight done. How long you think you'll be?" "We about an hour away now. So, give us until ten." "Aiight, one", Lacey said hanging up.

Hearing his conversation on the cellphone. All kinds of thoughts started to run through Animal's head. Being as though after he told Broke what went down. Broke hadn't said nothing since. Not asking any details or anything. Making Animal uneasy because of that hundred grand thing. He hoped he believed what he said about not being involved.

Broke could feel the tension in the air. That's why he purposely didn't ask any questions. In order to see what kind of reaction Animal had. He knew Animal for years and knew he was loyal. So he believed everything he said about the money thing. What he had an issue with was why Animal allowed it. It wasn't a big deal, but it still had to be put in perspective.

Breaking the silence Broke said, "Man, you my eyes and ears when I'm not around. Small things lead to big things. Ain't no telling what he might've tried next. If he lived to pull that shit off. Next time check niggas when they in violation. Silence is tantamount to condone."

Glad to hear Broke speak, Animal said, "Yeah you right. That's my bad. I looked at the situation like I'd be hating if I said something." "Yeah, I know fam. Ain't nobody perfect."

It wasn't that Animal was scared of Broke or nothing. It was just that he had mad love for him. And didn't want to be looked at like no snake. At thirty-two Broke was his senior by five years and he had a lot of respect for him. Truth be told, he played an Important role in bringing Broadie Boyz to its prominence, Hence his high-ranking status. Changing the subject Broke asked, "So what you think about Telly?" "I like that nigga he gangsta."

"Yeah me too. The nigga been holding it all the way down. Locking that new spot. Ima step him up tonight. His talents can be used on a bigger level." "I'm feeling that, "Animal remarked co-signing. "It's official then. Him and Petey."

"Yeah Petey been reppin for a minute. He just gotta get some age on him." The rest of the drive was in silence. Both men keeping their eyes on their surroundings. On point for an ambush. Knowing it was plenty more "Tone's" out there. Eager to take a shot at the leader of the notorious Broadie Boyz. Thirty minutes later, Animal pulled the truck in front of Lacey's Lounge. Jumping out, they headed inside out the rain.

Upstairs in the carpeted room where Lacey always stayed. Lounging on the expensive couches drinking down shots of liquor. Lacey, Petey, and Telly waited patiently on Broke's arrival. Occupying themselves with idle conversation. As rain from outside beat against the windows.

Sitting on the edge of his seat narrating one of his escapades. Petey said with animation, "So this nigga sitting at a stoplight, Playing his part too. I can't front....In a drop top five point O with some Versace shade on bumpin some Jay Z shit. Like his shit don't stink. You know what went through my mind when I saw him?"

Grinning because he liked Petey. Lacey played devil's advocate asking, "What?"

"Chi-Ching!", he yelled in response.

Both Lacey and Telly started to laugh. Then in the midst of their laughter, from across the room Broke appeared asking, "What's so funny?" "Oh yo, what's up Broke. Ain't shit, just tripping off the youngbuck here.", Lacey said.

Smiling Broke crossed the room and seated himself. Then helped himself to a drink from the corn liquor on the table. Pouring himself a healthy glass from the plastic jug. "What's up Telly?", he greeted before gulping down the liquor.

"Nothing much. Just enjoying myself, that's all."

At that moment, Animal appeared out the stairwell, crossing the room to where they sat. Flopping down on one of the couches with a sigh. Pouring himself another glass Broke said, "I done heard some good things about ya'll niggas. Especially you Telly. It's been what, about a little over a month and a half since you been down with us?"

"Yeah"

And already you shining fam. I like that yo. The standouts is the only ones I reward. I knew you was gonna turn out right. You been gangsta ever since I known you."

Very interested in where the conversation was going, Telly drank down his glass of liquor, Then placed it on the glass table. Giving Broke his undivided attention.

Taking a sip from his glass, Broke swished the strong liquor around in his mouth. After swallowing he said, "Personally, I think you done outgrown your current position. So I'm stepping you up. You heard?"

"Yeah", he said intrigued.

"From now on, you a two-star General. And you'll be assigned with me. Being as though Hakeem went and got himself killed. I know it's other niggas lurking. You alright with that?"

Staring Broke in his eyes he said, "Yeah no doubt."

"Good", he said leaning back and crossing his legs. "You'll take over Telly's spot Petey. I'm feeling your gangsta too."

Smiling Petey just nodded his head.

"Now somebody give me the full run down on our spot."

Clasping his hands together Lacey sat up. "Tone was basically the main resistance out there. Being as though he out the way now, it should be all good."

Speaking for the first time, Animal asked, "Them niggas that used to work for him. Do they know what time it is?"

Lacey shook his head up and down. "Yeah, they done already made a payment.

"How much?", Broke asked.

"Fifty Grand."

Looing over towards Telly, Broke said, "Go ahead and take that for yourself fam. You earned it. Consider it a perk with your promotion."

"Thank yo. I appreciate it gang. Word up. You ain't showed me nothing but love from day one."

At that moment right there. The last suspicion from his initiation night fell away. He just chalked it up as a dying man's plea. As well as a paranoid ex-con who just came home. Everything was all love as far as he was concerned. And for the rest of the night as they talked business. He was truly at ease.

It was past eleven o'clock by the time they finished meeting. Then afterwards, it took an additional thirty minutes for Telly yo drive home. Across the city in one of the hoopties the Broadie Boyz owned He still hadn't brought himself a car yet. Preferring to stack his dough. Feeling his first priority was to get his family out that roach infested apartment. Opening the door to their apartment. He walked inside with his black Columbia rain suit dripping. Closing the door behind him. Finding all the lights out. Which was normal considering the time. Then headed straight towards their bedroom. Waking Tanya unintentionally as he entered.

"Hey boo", she said in a low tone. "What's up", he said, heading for the dresser.

Once he reached it, he pulled out the bottom drawer. Pulled the fifty grand he was given by Broke out. Placed it in a hole inside the dresser on top of the other money he had saved. Then placed the drawer.

"What time is it?", Tanya asked.

"Ten past twelve."

"I'm starting to miss you boo. With all these late hours."

Slipping off his rain suit and clothes Telly said, "Oh really". "Yeah, you ain't never home."

"That money ain't just gonna walk to us. You got to go get it", he said climbing in bed.

"I still miss you", she stated turning over on her back.

Climbing over her naked body under the covers, Telly said, "Let me see if I can fix that."

Then he slowly started to kiss her. Running his hand down to her pussy. Inserting three of his fingers inside. Fingering her sex as he slid his mouth over her breasts. Sucking on her right nipple while gripping her other breast with his hand. Getting partially aroused from her obvious pleasure. Listening to her soft moans under his expertise.

"Mmmmm.... Put it in me Telly."

As he slid his fingers out from inside her. She cocked her firm sexy legs up by his side. Licking her luscious lips as he slowly slid inside her.

Savoring her warm wetness for a few seconds. Before starting to stroke with slow firm strokes. Making a clapping sound every time his balls hit her pussy. Causing her to lift her legs higher. Knocking the covers back as she placed her feet near his shoulder. "Fuck me harder."

Grabbing her pretty pedicured feet with his hands. Telly obliged by slamming himself harder and harder inside her. As she arched her back to meet his powerful strokes.

"Oooo-Oooo-Oooo....Yeah", she whispered while pulling her legs farther back.

Putting her elbows behind her knees. Gave Telly a full view of her shaved pussy. As he rammed it so hard. The bed started squeaking from their friction. Her breasts bouncing with every stroke until she succumbed to a powerful orgasm.

Switching positions by turning on her side. She lifted one leg up allowing Telly to re-enter her. Laying down behind her on his side. Telly continued to stroke. Kissing on her neck and palming her breasts, extending himself as far inside her as he could go.

"Yeah...Yeah...Come inside me boo...Hurry up...I'm cuming again."

Stroking faster he climaxed inside her just as she came for a second time.

Pulling out and laying behind her in spoon fashion. Telly held her close saying, "I love you so much."

"I love you too"

Inhaling her perfume scented body he said, "I got a surprise for you too."

"What is it!", she asked turning to face him.

"Tomorrow I want you to start looking for a home somewhere. We out of this shit hole. We ready."

Smiling she kissed him on the lips. Then in a show of happiness she slid down. Taking his dick inside her mouth..."

Part

2

Chapter 8

Staring at her reflection in the bathroom mirror. Tanya scrutinizes the application of peach lip gloss on her lips. Making sure she had applied it with perfection. Before heading out in her blue nurse uniform with matching clogs. Into the kitchen where Tahira sat eating her breakfast.

Through a mouth full of Captain Crunch cereal, Tahira said, "I need some lunch money."

"Ladies don't talk with their mouths", Tanya said firmly. "And anyway, what do you mean lunch money. Since when have you started buying lunch? We have plenty of peanut butter and bread for you to make some sandwiches." Mouth clear of food now she said, "Since Daddy been home. He was in such a rush to leave this morning, he forgot."

Knowing their excessive sex was the cause of him rushing, she blushed. "He gonna spoil you rotten. How much you need?" "Ten dollars."

Reaching in her bra, Tanya pulled out a roll of money. "Ten dollars! Girl you don't need that much for no lunch. I'm giving you five", she said peeling off a five-dollar bill and handing it to her.

"Five", she said turning her lips up.

"Yeah, five. And that's too much. You don't need to be eating all that junk food anyway. Because I know that's what you're buying. If you don't watch, you're gonna get fat."

Finishing off her cereal, Tahira hopped down from her seat. Walking over to the kitchen sink to place her bowl inside. While Tanya watched from behind shaking her head. Placing the roll of money back in her bra, Noticing how Tahira didn't even say thank you. Already used to Telly's special treatment of her. Taking for granted her blessings.

"Girl, you better count your blessings. This neighborhood is full of families who would love to be able to have peanut butter period", she lectured. "Now grab your bookbag and let' go before your late.

"I don't need no bookbag no more until next year. The teachers have already collected the books issued at the beginning of the year."

"Well, let's go."

Pausing for a second in the living room. She grabbed her black pocketbook and headed out the door. Followed by Tahira who carefully shut the door behind her. One step behind as they went down the staircase. On up outside the apartment building.

"Okay, I love you."

"I love you too."

Turning in opposite directions. They both headed their respective ways. One towards her elementary school and the other to her job as a nurse. Walking in a hospital located in North Philly named Temple University Hospital.

Sitting in a single seat on the subway train. With her stockinged legs crossed at the ankle. Looking through a copy of the Philadelphia Daily News. Searching inside for a home for sale. Tanya projected a pretty sight to any straight man in the vicinity. Sitting there with her tight nurse uniform hugging her curves. Exuding femininity through her every pore. Her physical beauty was flawless.

A teenager standing with his friends. Preparing to get off at the next stop. Displaying his best smile remarked, "I wish I was a nurse uniform. You need a youngbull?"

Hearing his comment, Tanya was flattered. Looking in his direction she looked him up and down. "No, I don't need a youngbull. But if you was a little older." Puffing his chest out, the teenager's smile got bigger. As he strutted towards the exit. Seeing the subway coming to a stop. Getting off, leaving Tanya giggling at his antics. She was glad she made his day because he made hers. No matter how much she was complimented. Which was a lot by all different ages of men. She always showed her appreciation to that person. Never letting it go to her head. Like so many women did. Knowing at age twenty-eight that she wouldn't be beautiful forever. Secretly hoping inside that she did though.

Getting back to her search of the newspaper. Her excitement from last night's news was evident in her wondering mind. No matter how hard she concentrated, she couldn't help thinking about the future. Remembering all the struggle she went through while Telly was locked up. Trying to keep her head above water. In hopes of giving Tahira more opportunity than she had coming up. Sometimes working two jobs just to provide for their needs.

Now for the first time in her life. She was getting ready to own her own home, and God knows what else. She'd seen all the money Telly had stashed in the house. Every time she did, it left her breathless. At just a little over a months' time, Telly made more money than she'd ever seen. She could just Imagine how much they'd have in the long run.

The sound of her stop being announced pulled her from her fantasy. Folding her newspaper in half, she headed towards the exit. Stepping onto the subway platform in the midst of a throng of people. Heading towards jobs as she was. Climbing the stairwell up towards the streets with reckless abandon. No regard for anyone in their way. As they rushed to make it to places of employment on time.

Back on the streets from underground. Traffic was busy from people doing their morning commute. Smells from hotdog vendors permeated the air. Crossing the street against the traffic light. Tanya first walked to the safety of a little island of cement centered in the street. Then from there over to the opposite sidewalk. Where one of the entrances was to the tall building, she worked for in Temple University.

Stepping through the double glass doors into the front lobby. She greeted the security man seated in front. "How you doing Mr. Kennedy?" "I'm fine now that I seen you. I was quite down until you came through the door.", the middle-aged man said flirtatiously.

Smiling, she responded, "You better stop before I tell your wife." "I ain't scared of that woman", he said with a serious face. "Yeah right", she said, pretending like she was headed to the section his wife worked in. Throwing up his hand in surrender in surrender he said, "Chill."

At that they both laughed. She then headed on towards her station located on the seventh floor of the building. Taking the elevator and making it there in a few minutes. Walking out the mechanical doors, just as her girlfriend Stacy was walking by. "What's up T?", Stacy said, stopping where she stood.

"Hey, ain't nothing. Tired that's all.", she answered walking over to log herself in. Smirking, Stacy said, "Ever since your man came home. Every morning you come to work tired. Damn girl, give the man a rest."

Logging herself in, Tanya giggled. "Shit, ain't no way. I gots to have mine. I can't resist him."

"Damn.", Stacy said mischievously. "So, when you gonna let me meet him. You always talking about him. The suspense is killing me. We could set up a double date or something. That way you could meet my new boyfriend too." "New boyfriend? You ain't never told me about no new boyfriend. What happened to Chris?"

Turning her lips up in disgust Stacy said, "Fuck that corny ass nigga. I got rid of his ass about a month ago. I'm glad I did too. Because if I didn't, I wouldn't have met Eric." "Damn, so what Chris do?"

"I just got tired of his corny ass. Doing the same shit over and over again. That shit got so boring after a while." "I know he's heartbroken. I believe he really loved you. So, tell me about this Eric."

"He tall and light-skinned with an athletic build. Handsome and keeps his hair in cornrows. And he owns his own restaurant down on South Street in South Philly. I met him there when me and my cousins was hanging out."

"Sounds interesting. How old is he?"

"Thirty-five."

"Good luck on keeping him. I'll check with Telly and see when we could double date.", she said, coming away from the logbook. "Now I got to do my rounds. I'll holler at you later on."

"Yeah, me too. See you later."

Walking in different directions down the hallway. Both women went to do their routine rounds. Which consisted of checking on patients in rooms. According to their assigned area given by their supervisor at the beginning of the week. All throughout the day they made continual rounds. Until going on break at lunchtime.

Sitting at a cafeteria table eating a turkey sandwich. Between bites Tanya continually glanced at the newspaper. Not really paying attention to what Stacy was saying.

"What is you looking for?", Stacy stopped mid-sentence. "You haven't heard a word I said, have you?" "I'm sorry Stacy. I'm trying to find something in the newspaper. I'm looking for a new place to live." "Another apartment?" "No, a house or maybe a condo. I haven't seen anything so far. That would be an ideal place to live." "What you looking for? It's some homes for sale out in South Philly where I live."

Looking up at her from the newspaper she turned her lips. "Please, I'm not trying to move from one crime ridden area to another. I might as well stay in Susquehanna if I moved out there where you stay. I'm looking for a safe environment for my daughter to come up in. At the same time, not predominately white suburbs. So my daughter don't grow up around a bunch of which people. You know what I'm saying?"

"Yeah I feel you."

Turning the pages in between bites of her sandwich. Tanya continued to look until the remainder of her break. Finding out the last final minutes some homes that were to her liking. Placing a circle with her pen around them for future reference. Then, after dumping the wrappings of her lunch in the trash. She headed back to her station on the seventh floor.

Driving one of Broke's personal care slowly through the streets. Telly was enjoying himself in the sleek, silver colored Mercedes E Class he borrowed. Starting to really feel the urge to buy some wheels. Being as though he now had more time to spend with his family. Finding out earlier this morning. That his new responsibilities in the organization. Weren't as heavy as his previous position was. Pulling a lot of late hours on the regular.

Basically, now he played a bodyguard role occasionally concerning Broke. Filling the slot that Hakeem's death left. The majority remainder of his responsibilities on the other hand. Were playing the manager role at a few Barbershops and a restaurant. That were owned by the Broadie Boyz in the city. Enabling him to be able to put on a front. In order to hide the money he was making. He also gave direction to any plan that came down the line.

Stopping at the stoplight at 22nd & Diamond street in front of the projects. He felt like a superstar with all eyes on him. Watching in admiration and envy. The luxury car poised to take off like a rocket. As soon as the light turned green. Which it did in a matter of seconds. Sending him on towards his next stop for the day. Before he picked up Tanya to go check on some houses. Double parking out directly in front of the Barbershop. He put his blinkers on, tucked his 9mm pistol in his pocket, then climbed out. Leaving the music still pumping out the open car windows. Simply because it was only going to take a few minutes to handle business.

Walking in between two parked cars. A couple of steps across the sidewalk brought him to the Barbershop entrance. A place called Razor Sharp. Opening the glass doors and going in. He was greeted by the sight of a packed place. Having each Barber busy cutting hair at their stations.

Stepping towards the short dark-skinned barber nearest the door. Telly asked, "Which one of you is John? I'm the new manager for Razor Sharp from chises." Looking him up and down. The short dark-skinned barber said, "That'll be me. I'll be with you in one minute. Let me finish this guy's shape up." Not feeling like waiting, but having no choice, Telly turned to lookout the windows. Keeping his eye on the open window Mercedes outside. As the barber's so called one minute, ended up turning into five minutes.

Done with the man's shape up. After taking his pay from his customer. John turned towards Telly with an outstretched hand. "Sorry about that man. It's always real busy on Friday's. You know how it is. Everybody wanting to look their best for the weekend."

Shaking his hand Telly responded, "It's no problem. I understand."

As a superior of that Barbershop on that street. John collected all the money from his co-workers. That was to be paid for the rental of their space once a month. Giving it to the manager as he came through. "Here you go Telly. That's twenty-four hundred for all eight of us here.", John said handing him a roll of bills. Counting the money real quick. Seeing that it was all there. Telly said while pocketing the money, "Aiight John, see you next time. Any problems you know how to reach me right?"

"Yeah"

"Take it easy", Telly said walking back out the door to the car. Climbing inside he pulled off in a matter of seconds. Taking a left at the corner bringing the car back on Diamond. Cruising down several blocks before making another left at 16th & Susquehanna. Heading towards his three-story apartment building.

Pulling up out front he beeped the horn several times. Until finally Tanya came walking out and climbing in. Giving him a kiss on his lips saying, "Hey." "So where to?", he asked to putting the car back in motion. "Well I got several places I done marked off. We'll start with the ones in North Philly first. There's only one I had to contact a real estate agent for." "And where is that one at?"

"Way out in Chestnut Hill. Up by Wadsworth Avenue."

"Ay shit. You want to stay way out there?"

"I don't know. Let's just see it first before we prejudge", she said pulling a little piece of paper out her pocketbook. Looking it over twice before saying, "The first spot is out in Nicetown on Bouvier street."

"Bouvier street here we come", he said playfully. "What's up Tahira?" "Oh, she at my mother's house for the weekend. I decided to take advantage of this new free time you have", she said with a raised eyebrow.

"You a goddamn freak yo!"

Giggling she said, "And you silly." Then for the first time started to take in the interior design. "I like this."

Smiling at her comment. That there made the decision final concerning a car. It was one thing for him to consider flossing. Another when either Tanya or his daughter wanted something. It felt good to him to make up for his absence. As long as it didn't hurt the proverbial bank. All they had to do was ask and it was theirs.

"What's wrong?", Tanya asked, while twirling her wineglass in her hand. Having finished surveying homes about an hour ago. Coming to a final decision on the most expensive one. Falling in love with the spacious home on sight. Despite the small reservations they had concerning other issues. They sat now in an upscale restaurant named Morimoto. Where the seats the patrons sat in glowed and changed colors slowly.

"Nothing really. I'm just thinking on what kind of effect this environment gonna have on Tahira. Living in the hood has its plus side too."

"I know. I was thinking about the same thing earlier when I was searching for homes. I know a lot of black people who grew up in that type of environment as Chestnut Hill. Most of them seem to be out of touch with reality. Not understanding our plights as a race. Thinking its all good for us in America."

Sitting up in the booth chair. Telly leaned on the table with his elbows. "Exactly I know. I don't want Tahira to grow up thinking like that. But on the other hand I don't want her in an environment we grew up in either. Shit is crazy right."

"Yeah, it definitely is."

Turning his head and looking towards the kitchen area. Telly said, "Goddamn where is the food at. Fuck around and spaz out in here. I'm hungry than a muthafucka."

Smiling with a shocked look on her face she said, "You better not Telly. Don't embarrass me."

Grabbing the edge of the table with a serious look. He acted as if he was getting ready to flip it over. Strain showing all over his face as he lifted upwards. "Fuck that it's on."

There wasn't no way he was gonna flip the table. Simply because it was attached to the wall. The look in his face made her laugh. "You are so silly. Stop playing."

"Oh, you think it's for play?", he said taking his hands off the table's edges. Then grabbing the basket of biscuits sitting on the table. He flipped the remaining biscuits onto the wooden floor stating, "I'm tired of eating that shit."

Laughing at his antics. Very quickly she leaned down to gather up the biscuits. Before anyone noticed what happened. "Boy you are so crazy." Grabbing the saltshaker, he made as if to flip it too. Before he could, she grabbed his hands laughing hysterically. The people around them stared out of curiosity. Trying to find out what was so funny. At that precise moment their waitress started walking towards them holding a tray. Seeing her approach Telly said, "They lucky."

Placing their plates of food in front of them. The waitress asked, "Is everything okay?"

"Yes, thank you very much.", Tahira replied.

"Okay, enjoy your meal.", she said walking away.

Biting into his sirloin steak with gusto. Tanya just smiled at his silliness. Getting started on her meal as well. Reminiscent about when they were in Benjamin Franklin High School. How she was attracted to him because he made her laugh. Being in total contrast with the reputation he had in the neighborhood. Unlike most guys with the same notorious reputation. Who portrayed the Image if being a hardcore twenty-four/seven. No matter what the circumstances.

He was the male she gave her virginity to. After six months of holding out on him. Trying to make sure that wasn't all he wanted. Now many years later. She was real appreciative of her hesitation. Having right there in front of her, living proof. That showed how good of a decision she made. Feeling that his love was just as strong now. As it was on that first day.

Then just at that particular moment in her thoughts. Whether by coincidence or some kind of freak intervention. When she looked up her whole demeanor instantly changed. Coming in the front door of the restaurant with a woman in tow. Was a man she fell in love with while Telly was locked up. Only pushing him away about a month and a half before Telly's release. Not because she wasn't in love with him anymore. But because she felt her place was at Telly's side regardless, Simply because she had a baby by him. She couldn't believe her luck. Of all the places they could have ate. Her ex ended up eating at the same place as her. On the same day and at the same time. Trying to avoid his attention. She moved her body in such a way as to hide in front of Telly. Where if he happened to look he couldn't see her. It was a millisecond too late though. He'd seen her and now was headed in their direction. Holding the woman's hand as he came.

Walking past their table slowly he said, "What's up Tanya? How you been doing?"

Hearing a man's voice speaking to his girl smooth like. Telly whipped his head to see who it was. Any playfulness that was in his expression before completely gone now.

"I'm doing fine. How you doing Greg?" "Good"

"Greg this here is my BOYFRIEND Telly", she said with an emphasis on the word "boyfriend."

Noddin his head in greeting he said, "And this is a friend of mine named Wanda."

She nodded noticing the tension in the air. Feeling uncomfortable she said, "Nice to meet you all, "Then pulled Greg down the aisle with her."

While they were still in earshot Telly asked loudly, "Who the fuck is that? Stopping at our table speaking to you in my presence."

Knowing how quick Telly could switch faces from silly to vicious. She hurried to calm the situation before it blew up. "Just some dude I know. Calm down."

"Hell naw. I ain't like the sounds of that nigga voice. When he spoke to you. Where you know him from?"

Deciding to tell the halfway truth he said, "He's the cousin of one of my girlfriends I work with. I met him at one of her get togethers a couple of years ago."

Calming down a little at her explanation. Still starring at Greg as he walked away. He said, "Oh".

Getting back to eating their food in silence completely now. They both finished up the remainder of their meal quickly. Both eager to leave such an uncomfortable situation.

Seeing their waitress taking orders from another table. Telly turned in his booth saying rudely, "Check yo."

"One moment sir", she said irritated at his rude tone.

As soon as she finished taking the peoples order. She went to get his bill. Taking his payment on the spot with a big tip. Forgotten in a instant his rudeness. As they both got up to leave.

Chapter 9

The weekend they spent alone together flew by. As time was wont to do when a person was having fun. During their brief hiatus from their normal lifestyles. They roamed the city almost in its entirety. Visiting spots, they frequented when they were teenagers. Reliving the past as they shared tales of old memories. From the 69th street Upper Darby movie together to the Arcades down on 40th Street. Right now, it was the beginning of the week. And from last night's persuasive debate with Telly. Where his argument came out on top. Instead of reporting in for work as usual. Tanya was driving their new red colored 745 B.M.W. That was brought the past weekend. Towards a furniture store she knew about. In order to be able to deck out their new home before the week was out.

Like Telly she wanted to get out the apartment as soon as possible too. She just didn't think it should be this quick. Being as though Tahira still had some days of school left. In the end she had lost out though. When Telly pointed out that they weren't teaching nothing anyway. As well as the fact that he was the man of the house, and she needed to do as she was told.

Smiling her pretty signature smile, She thought about the tricks she performed in bed shortly afterwards. Getting Telly to admit at that time. That she was the one who really ran shit. Grinning the whole time as she pleasured him with her mouth. Happy to please her man. Who in such a short time had given her so much.

Making a right off Passyunk Avenue. She drove the Beemer towards the furniture store she was going to. Pulled up inside its street parking lot. Then climbed out and headed to the entrance of Furniture U.S.A. In order to see what kind of good deals it had to offer. Mentally already thinking of another furniture store she knew. Just in case the prices they offered weren't to her satisfaction.

Walking into the air-conditioned room felt good on her exposed skin. Immediately to her a living room set caught her attention. As she walked in its direction. Somewhere farther back in the store. She heard someone call her name, causing her to instantly turn in that direction. Only to find to her complete amazement. For the second time in four days her ex-boyfriend Greg. Although this time he was alone. Carrying in his arms a television set to a counter. Sitting it down for the clerk to ring up. Then strolling over to where she stood.

Looking at her in her Prada dress with matching stiletto sandals and purse, Greg complimented, "You look good yo."

"Thanks."

"I see why you pushed a nigga to the curb. I could never afford to buy you things like that."

Not knowing what to say she said, "You know it ain't nothing like that. You know exactly why I did what I did."

"True dat, but I still don't like it. I can't turn my feelings off and on."

Trying to change the subject she said, "So tell me this. How is it I've managed to bump into you twice in the last two days?"

Not going to let her off that easy. He directed the conversation back where he wanted it. "Fate, that's how. It must be meant to be."

Letting that statement hang in the air for a second. Wondering at the truth in those words she said, "Well it was nice seeing you again. But I'm on a tight schedule and really don't have too much time to waste. Take care of yourself", she said turning towards the living room set.

Getting upset now at her cold display. A woman who he knew still loved him, he said, "Hold up man. Why are you treating me like this? I haven't done anything to deserve such treatment. How you just gonna flip on me because I love you? What kinda shit is that? You know that ain't right."

Emotions running wild now from his words, she spun back around to face him. "Don't try to fucking guilt trip me. You knew way beforehand that the father of my daughter was locked up. And I still loved him and still wanted him in my life. How was I supposed to know we would fall in love? What you doing right now isn't right. You knew the rules just like me", she said in a huff. "You think it's any easier for me?"

Understanding that what she said was the truth. Some of the aggression receded from his next words. "You right, I'm sorry. Like I say I can't tun my feelings off and on. I think about you all the time."

"You've been on my mind lately as well."

"This shit is torture yo. Word up", he said with distressed look. Then suddenly he looked up as if he had just caught a bright idea. "Okay, I'll tell you what. It's obvious our feelings are the same concerning what we think of each other. But as you pointed out I knew the rules. And I'm telling you straight up, right now. I can respect your position. But does that mean we can't be friends?"

A long moment of silence passed before she answered. "Yeah, I don't see nothing wrong with that. Just as long as you play by the rules."

Smiling seeing that he had made some progress he said, "Deal them. How about I treat you to some lunch. That is if your schedule permits. Let's go and smash out some chicken cheesesteaks."

Knowing she had no schedule to keep. To stay in sync with the lie she told she said, "Yeah I think I have some time. I need to finish my business here first though."

"By all means, don't let me hold you up. Let me get back to this T.V. set I'm buying. And let you handle yours."

Parting company they both went back to their previous doings. Thoughts in both their minds in what direction they were headed as "friends".

Standing out front of their spacious new home. With Tahira piggyback style and Tanya to his side. Telly directed a question to his daughter. "So how you like it? What you think?"

"It's big", she answered.

Laughing Telly said, "And that's just the view from outside. Wait until you see the inside. Your bedroom aloe us half the size of that apartment."

"But daddy?", she asked innocently.

"What?"

"How come it ain't nobody outside? Everybody outside the way. Where is everybody at?"

Knowing how difficult change was for anyone, especially children. Telly had anticipated and was prepared for her comparisons. "They around, trust me. Around here, they have a lot of afterschool facilities for kids. Recreational gyms and indoor swimming pools. Unlike back down Susquehanna. So that's probably where everybody's at. They even have a performing arts after school program. Where they teach poetry, acting, and music too. So, you can get some help with your poetry you like to do. You'll see. For now, let's go check out your bedroom."

Walking up the front brick staircase. When they made it to the large steel front door. Tanya pulled the door key out of her Prada purse and opened the door. Seconds later, they all filed onto the beige carpeted floor. Heading across it and up the wooden staircase. Towards the upstairs bedroom Telly promised to show her. When they reached it, Telly put his daughter down. Watching in satisfaction the look on her face as she explored the large room. Looking inside her carpeted bedroom walk-in closet. Then over to the electrical fireplace that every room was equipped with. Touching the fake fire logs that were laying inside. Then finally she walked over to the window in her room. Standing on tiptoes looking out at their backyard. Eyes instantly focused on a blue colored trampoline.

"Who's tramboline?"

Correcting her, Tanya said, "It's pronounced trampoline."

"Who's trampoline?"

Telly said, "It's yours. The people we brought the house from has a daughter about your age. So being as though they couldn't take it with them. They left it after finding we had a daughter too."

"Can I go play on it?"

Looking concerned about her daughter jumping on that thing. Tanya looked towards Telly expressing that. Ignoring Tanya's look he said, "I don't see why not."

Smiling Tahira ran out of the room. Navigating her way through the house to the backyard. In minutes they could see her flying in the air. Flipping over and over on top of the trampoline.

"She don't need to be playing on no shit like that. That thing looks real dangerous. What if she misses it on her way down?"

"Stop worrying. She straight. I told you she was gonna like it. Did you see the look on her face as she was exploring? I give her one summer and she'll be over Susquehanna." Telly said nodding his head.

"Yeah, I agree."

"Well, its official as of today. I put the down payment on it this morning. How things go with the furniture?"

Feeling kind of guilty at the mention of that. Because she had lunch with Greg. Even though all they did was eat and talk she answered, "It's all good. I got everything we could possibly need. That old stuff at the apartment, we'll give to goodwill. Our stuff should be delivered here by Wednesday."

"You paid the whole payment?"

"Yeah"

"That's good. Cause it ain't no need to be making payments on that shit. We just got to do the house like that. So, we don't draw no attention. That's the kind of shit put the feds on a nigga ass."

Grabbing her around the waist and palming her bare ass cheeks underneath her Prada dress. Telly said, looking at Tahira in the backyard. "Let's break this new home in real quick. Before Tahira come back in."

Smiling she wrapped her arms around him. Sticking her tongue in his mouth saying in between kisses. "And-You-Call-Me-A-Freak." Pulling back, she walked over towards the fireplace. Pausing only to slide her thong down over top of her stilettos. Before leaning forward with both palms on the walls. Exposing her pretty round ass as her dress hiked up around her waist. Looking back at Telly smiling and twisting her waist for effect. Walking up behind her, Telly unbuckled his pants swiftly. Sliding two fingers inside her pussy as his pants dropped to his ankles. Fingering her wetness for a couple of seconds. Before sliding his dick inside. Palming both her ass cheeks, while slamming all his weight up against her.

Losing her balance from his vigorous thrusts. Tanya slid her feet out of her sandals. Then, standing barefoot on the carpeted floor. Leaned over grabbing an ankle with one hand. While bracing against the wall with the other. Exposing more of herself for Telly's hard strokes.

"Ummmm-Yeah-Fuck me harder-Umm-Oooo-harder-harder", she said out of breath.

Obliging, Telly pistoned inside her as hard as he could. The slap of flesh on flesh loudly echoed in the empty room. Until suddenly, he exploded inside her warmth. Emptying himself with closed eyes. Smiling at the so called, "breaking in", of their new home.

Chapter 10

"Ahh shit! That sneaky bitch! Jack gonna fuck that bitch up yo! Watch what I tell you!", the teenager yelled in his hospital room. Laying in a bed on the other side of the room. A young man around the corner same age piped in. "No doubt fam. That chick fucking with the wrong muthafucka."

They were both patients in Temple University Hospital in bed eating lunch watching a soap opera called "The Young and the Restless." Recovering from gunshot wounds occurring in two different locations.

Coming inside the room to make her rounds. Tanya heard the last mans remark. "Who fucking with the wrong muthafucka?", she asked with a smirk. Looking over at her smiling. The one that made the comment said, "Oh, this chick on T.V. She trying to snake my man, Jack. On some Willie bobo shit. Trying to son him like he Joe Joe Sausage head. It ain't going down like that though.

His roommate with a serious look on his face. Nodded his head vigorously in full agreement.

Sweeping her eyes across them both. She suddenly broke out in a bigger grin. "You know what ya'll two look and sound like? Two old bitties in a retirement home. Sitting in here watching soap operas. I thought ya'll was thugs."

At that they all burst out in fits of laughter, Then one of them in typical teenage browado said, "Shit, ain't nothing else to watch. And anyway, I'm secure in my gangsta. I ain't got to be on no hard core shit all day." "Me either", the other one piped in.

Giggling she said, "Aiight, secure in my gangsta and me either. Ya'll finish with them trays?"

Smiling they said yes. So, she went towards their beds to gather them up. Her beautiful shape carefully watched by one or the other. Whenever they were sure she wasn't looking. Then, on her way out she stopped to ask, "Either one of ya'll need something before I go?"

The one nearest the doorway said, "You saying that like you ain't coming back."

"I'm not. I only gotta work a half a day today. So I'll see ya'll tomorrow. Do ya'll need anything?"

"Naw, I'm good."

"Yeah, we straight."

"Aiight then ya'll. Have a nice day and be good okay."

Heading out the doorway on down the hallway. Tanya walked towards the food cart to get rid of her burden. As she placed the trays inside, Stacy appeared a few seconds later performing the same thing.

Out of breath Stacy stated, "Girl I'm pooped. My feet and back are killing me. When I get off of work today, I'm going straight to sleep." Teasing her, Tanya bragged. I feel sorry for you. I'm getting ready to do just that. As soon as I log out in a few minutes."

Playing with her back. Stacy said in her best slave impression. "Fuck you um a miss B.M.W. driving suburbanite. Us um poor folk round the way can't afford to take half days whenever we want.

Smiling, Tanya said before walking away, "You crazy. I'll see you tomorrow."

"Yeah alright be safe.", Stacy said to her fleeing form.

Logging herself out, Tanya took the elevator down to the bottom floor. Went inside a bathroom to change her clothes. From out of her nurse uniform into a Dolce and Gabbana skirt outfit with some slingbacks. Then she headed to the garage area. Hopping in the 745 and heading towards her destination. Which was yet another rendezvous with her ex-Greg. Something that had become a routine ever since their meeting in the furniture store.

Navigating the Beemer through traffic. Tanya thought about where her relationship with Greg was headed...Ever since that meeting about a month ago. Almost every day, except weekends, they got together and spent a few hours together as "friends". Either on her lunch break or half days. Which was something she started increasing by talking on the regular. With all the money that Telly was brining in on a daily basis.

At this particular point. Her and Greg had been able to maintain the standard they set. Nothing physical as of to date had taken place. Slowly but surely, that barrier was beginning to erode though. Being in each other's presence so often. Naturally sent them both into flashbacks of each others sexual expertise. Causing Tanya to question her better judgement. Flirting mentally with the idea of having her cake and eating it too. Men did it all the time, she thought. For further justification in this line of thinking. She told herself that sex was one thing. While what she had going on with Telly was another. In this months time of comparison between Greg and Telly. She knew and understood that she could never be with Greg. What her and Telly had was too strong. It didn't mean she wasn't human though. Having attractions for another man. At the same time, nothing would ever come between her love for Telly. She knew that just as well as she knew her name. So why not have a little fun?.....

Sitting at a table situated in a corner. Inside a restaurant that was located inside of the Adams Mark Hotel. Greg sat with his long legs stretched out. Drinking down a glass of Coke and patiently watching the entrance. For signs of Tanya's arrival who was about ten minutes late. According to his cheap looking swatch watch.

Figuring he might as well order for them both. Turning towards his waitress who was wiping down a table. He said, "Bridgette, I'm ready to order." Stopping what she was doing. She headed over with pen and pad in hand. "Alright Sir. What'll it be?"

Ordering both meals he sat back continuing to wait. Periodically glancing at his watch and looking towards the entrance. Finally, twenty-five minutes after the agreed upon time, Tanya came walking through the open doorway. Scanning around the restaurant until her eyes found him. Seated in the corner with a look of disappointment on his face.

Knowing his notorious impatience. She said while taking a seat across from him. " Sorry about that, I got caught up in traffic. They had some kind of accident on Girard Avenue. That had traffic backed up for forty-five minutes. How you doing?"

"I'm good. Cant complain too much. I already ordered our food about an half and hour ago. I hope you in the mood for some pig feet."

"Pig feet", she blurted out with disgust. Then looking around at the makeup of the restaurant, she knew he was joking. Laughing she said, "Stop playing." "Yeah, that's what you get. You should have seen your face. Next time, get here on time.", he said with a smile.

Getting comfortable in her seat. She crossed her legs at the knee under the table. "So, what's the word on your promotion at the job?", she asked. Referring to his job as a mail clerk.

"I haven't heard nothing yet. But I'm starting to have doubts."

"Stop thinking negative. You say a guy with the same background as you got promoted a while ago. So why would you doubt your chances."

"I'm not being negative. I'm just keeping it real with myself. If I can't keep it real with myself, who can I keep it real with? See number one, that guy that got promoted was white. So, you know how that go. The only thing I got to offer is my loyalty to the company. Being as though I've been working there ever since I was twenty-one. And that really ain't nothing. I've done some research too. Ninety-nine percent of the people that work in the department I'm trying to ger in at least have a bachelor's degree. "

Feeling what he was saying because she could relate. Knowing how hard it was for people without college education to get jobs period. She just gave him words of encouragement. "You never know though. You just might be that one percent." Continuing on in small talk. The way friends do when they're together. They talked until and throughout their whole meal. Enjoying each other's company. As they munched on some pasta with fettuccini sauce and garlic bread. Then, after finishing off glasses of ice cream for dessert. They relaxed in their seats. While waiting for the check to arrive.

"Damn, that was a lot of food.", Tanya said, with one hand on her stomach.

"Yeah, I know it. I ain't even know they got down like that. A homeboy put me onto this joint."

"We got to come here more often. I'm feeling this place."

"I'm feeling any place I'm at with you, period."

Looking him in the eyes. Tanya said flirtatious, "Is that so?"

"Yeah, you know that. What other kind of nigga would be content like I am. With just enjoying your company whenever I can."

"But are you really content?", she asked seriously.

Seeing the serious expression on her face. He wondered where she was headed with this line of questioning. "Honestly speaking, that answer would be no. Content that at least I'm still in your life. But you know how I really want it to be.", he said, pausing for effect. "So that makes me wonder. Why would you ask me that? You know you ain't never got to hide nothing from me. Just give it to me raw. What's up?"

Blurting it all out before she lost her nerve. She said, "I want my cake and eat it too. Can you deal with that?"

Laughing he said, "You had me scared as hell for a minute yo. I thought you was gonna say some fuck shit. Now let me get this right. What you saying is this: You want to step our relationship up, but I'm still on the low. Is that right?"

"Yeah"

Knowing this was gonna happen sooner or later. Feeling as though it was just a matter of time before she was all his again. He smiled saying, "I'm with it."

Minutes later, their waitress came with the bill. He paid the tab since it was turn. Then hand in had they walked to the front desk. In order to get a room. So they could both do something they been wanting to do for a while now...

Chapter 11

Sitting at a table for four with chairs turned towards the stage with Champagne chilled on ice in front of them. On a double date, Stacy and Tanya laughed uncontrollably at the antics of the comedian in front of them. While Telly and Eric laughed with restraint. Being as though the joke was made about men.

They were at a Comedy Club in downtown Philly. One of three places of entertainment they had planned for the night. With Telly and Eric halving the bill down the middle. Holding no luxury back for the women in their lives. Already just at the first stop spending over a grand. Looking over at Tanya laughing beside him Telly said, 'Shut the fuck up, It ain't that funny.'

Looking as if in shock at his words, but knowing he was playing, she responded, "No, you shut the fuck up."

Turning his attention back towards the stage. He made no response as she stared him down. She smiled to herself every time he cut his eyes her way. Then. Just a few minutes later the comedian told a joke about women. Sending Eric and Telly into a fit of laughter. Exaggeration in their laugh just to get on the women nerves.

Smiling at the faces Telly was making. Tanya playfully punched him in his stomach. "Cut that shit out." she said still smiling.

"Oh, you can laugh, but I can't. What part of the game is that? The shit was funny."

"Whatever."

Watching both of them from where she was sitting. Stacy said, "Ya'll two a trip. I can tell just from this little time seeing ya'll together. Ya'll made for each other without a doubt." Looking at Tanya in the eyes she asked, "How long ya'll been together again?"

"Twelve years", Telly blurted out.

Turning her head around quickly to look at him. Tanya said with a jerk of her neck. "It's thirteen. Remember when we was in the tenth grade?"

Telly paused for a second and thought. "Oh yeah, my bad. Anyway, twelve, thirteen same thing. Let's just say a long goddamn time."

"Everybody burst into laughter at the comment. Then Stacy said, "she talks about you all the time. Or at least when she comes to work these days. Now I know why."

Hiding her guilty look by pouring herself another glass of champagne. Tanya immediately explained herself before the unintentional seed Stacy planted could grow. "Yeah, now that Telly's home to help out, I don't need to work as hard as I did before. Thank God for that too."

"I can feel that girl. If you don't mind me asking Telly. What kind of work you do?"

For a second, Telly got real curious at Stacy's statement. Wondering why Tanya never told him about working a light schedule. Then, Tanya's explanation put him at ease. The thought of Tanya doing something sinister never crossed his mind. Simply because she wasn't that type of woman. Or so he thought.... "I'm a manager of a couple of different spots. Barbershops and a restaurant." He answered.

Joining the conversation, Eric said, "Word? I'm also a manager at a restaurant I own. It's a soul food joint out South Philly named after me." "Aiight, the place I'm at the same. It's called, Food for the Soul, located in North Philly. Right off of Spring Garden."

"Sounds like a nice place.", Stacy chimed in. "We might just drop by and check it out sometime."

Suddenly, applause broke out around the room. A signal that the comedian booked for the night was finished his set. Simultaneously the stage lights went out as he exited. Leaving the spacious room lightly dimmed. Setting the atmosphere for patrons to continue their night in conversation and alcohol. Glancing at his Rolex watch on his left wrist.

Telly asked, "So what's up ya'll? Ya'll want to go the club first. Then bust a grub afterwards. Or ya'll want to eat first?"

"Might as well eat first. Then burn off them pounds on the dance floor", Tanya said.

"Yeah, that makes sense", Stacy cosigned.

Standing up together the couples headed towards the exit. Stepping outside to the black limo waiting by the curbside. Ready to take them to the next destination of the night.

Finished eating dinner at a four-star restaurant. The couples climbed out of the limousine right near the club entrance. All eyes were on them as they walked past people waiting in line. Up towards the velvet rope where a beefy bouncer stood guard. Preoccupied trying to crack on a pretty woman standing in front of him. Trying to use her womanly charms to gain any advantage.

Red quarter length Gator boots echoing on the sidewalk. Telly came to a stop at the front. "Yo, what up Mal?"

Taking his attention from the woman. The beefy bouncer turned to see who was calling him. Then immediately started watching the velvet rope. "What's up Telly? How you fam?"

"I'm aiight yo. Just out having a good time." Then waving his hand across his entourage he said, "This here is my shorty Tanya and associates Stacy and Eric. Ya'll got some room up in the V.I.P.?"

"How ya'll doing?", he said nodding his head. "We should. If not, then somebody just got to get the fuck out. Ya'll go ahead on in. Vic 'll set ya'll straight."

Monitoring Tanya, Stacy, and Eric to go in first. As they filed past him while Mal closed back the velvet rope. He hung back with Mal for a few seconds. "Everything alright?", he asked seriously.

"Yeah, its all good. You know how we do.", Mal said making two letter B's with his fingers.

Patting Mal on his beefy back. Telly said while walking in. "Aiight then fam. Take it easy."

Stepping through the front corridor inside club "Triple Five". Looking around Telly could see it was almost packed to capacity. It was a grown and sexy club owned by the Broadie Boyz. That's why he had no problem gaining admittance. While others not in the know stood restlessly in a long line outside. Teased by the music bumping hot eighties jams. Hoping for a chance to get in one of the city's livest nightclubs.

Looking ahead and seeing a bouncer about to pat down Tanya. Telly called out from behind. "They with me Vic. That's my wifey right there and her friends."

Seeing where the voice was coming from. Vic stepped back. "Oh. My bad fam. Funny seeing you here."

Smiling, Telly walked up and shook the young mans hand. "Yeah, surprise nigga. I come to get my pop lock on."

"Get the fuck out of here.", Vic said laughing. "Ya'll got some room in the V.I.P. section?"

"Yeah you know it. Ya'll just follow me.", Vic said, leading the way towards V.I.P. "What ya'll be having to drink?"

"Some Cristal will be good.", Telly said.

Going up the stairway to the second level. They followed Vic into a less crowded section with dimmer lights then the rest of the club. Taking some seats towards the back. On a circular leather sofa situated around a glass table. Where they had a clear view of most of the club.

"Aiight fam. The spirits will be up in a flash. Enjoy yourself, everything's on the house.", Vic said with a smile. Then headed back down to his area. Impressed by the treatment Telly received, Stacy asked, "You come here often?"

"No, actually this my first time. Figured I'd come through and enjoy some hospitality. The person that owns this place is like family. We grew up together.", he said, telling half the truth.

"Oh"

Playing on the speakers overheard could be heard a popular eighties jam. "Your love...So good...Deserves an Encore...De-ser-ves an Encore...Your love...Ooh Ooo...So good...Deserves an Encore...De-ser-ves an En-core."

Rocking her body to the rhythm in dark colored Fendi outfit. Tanya sang, "When I had you to myself...That's my shit. Let's dance Telly."

Stepping out in the aisle immediately beside them in V.I.P., Telly and Tanya danced to that particular song. As well as five more afterwards.

Somehow ending up at the other end of the V.I.P. section. Until Telly begged off for a Cristal break. Leading Tanya by the hand back to their seats. Where Stacy and Eric sat hugged up talking. Stacy already looking more than tipsy. Sitting down Telly poured them both a glass. "This spot alright. I see why they say it be jumping. That D.J. ill wit it. Word Up!"

Between sips of her drink Tanya said, "Yeah I know it." Then glancing over towards Stacy she said, "You just gonna sit there all night?"

Speaking alittle slurred speech Stacy answered, "He can't dance."

Laughing, Telly encouraged. "Shit me either. Who gives a fuck. Dance with your shorty yo."

Feeling kind of embarrassed for being put on the spot. Also at the same time feeling a little courage from the alcohol. Downing another glass Eric said, "Fuck it."

Smiling they both got up and headed out the V.I.P. section. Down to the dance floor on the first level leaving Telly and Tanya alone. Drinking down his glass. Afterwards Telly just grabbed the whole bottle. Being as though it was another sitting still unopened. Then placed it to his lips and guzzled. Taking down a healthy swallow before putting it down. Enjoying the head rush he got. "You enjoying yourself?" ,he asked staring at her. Leaning up to kiss him on the lips. Her reply was simply, "Um Hmm."

"Good. That's really all I care about. You know that?" She nodded in understanding.

With thoughts of comfort in her mind. He probed back to earlier at the Comedy Club. Concerning her not going to work. Not because he thought something was up. But because he was curious. "So, what's up with the job you got. You tired of working there or something? Because if you want to, you know you ain't got to do shit. I'm holding the fort." Her guilty conscience made her pick her words carefully. "Now, it ain't nothing like that. I love being a nurse. It's just now, I don't have to worry and work so hard. So I do me."

Completely trusting he said with a smile. "Spending up all the money on clothes and shit."

On the defense, the way guilty people are, she said irritably, "Not all like that. I run errands too."

Peeping her tone and body language, Telly said in astonishment. "Calm down yo. I was just fucking with you. You know I don't care about that shit. As long as you happy."

Drinking down the rest of the Cristal in her glass. In order to calm her nerves. At that particular moment she started to feel real bad about her affair. Seeing how much Telly loved and trusted her. Then here she was doing what she did. Whether because of the intoxicants or something else. More than ever she felt confused.

"You want to dance some more?", she asked eager to do anything.

Grabbing her by the hand and bottle of Cristal by the other. They headed on down to the first level. To dance on the dance floor with Stacy and Eric. Switching up with each other and having a good time.

Chapter 12

"Check it out people! I'm telling you something good! Hallmark ain't got nothing on my joints! If you want to impress a loved one, friend, whoever! Make them feel special! I'm the one you need to see! I can even make one right here on the spot! Hallmark can't do that!" The young man yelled to passersby's. Coming out of the jewelry store located on Erie Avenue. Holding a small bf with a gold link chain inside. Tanya heard the young man's sales pitch from halfway down the Avenue. Where he stood against a brick wall beside a wool blanket. That was spread on the ground displaying his homemade cards.

Intrigued by his boots she headed in his direction. The late August sun beaming down on her now sun-tanned skin. As she navigated through the crowded sidewalk. Dressed in a Moschino skirt outfit with a matching sleeveless top and sandals. Moschino sunglasses protecting her eyes from the sun. Looking with approval on the homemade cards laying in neat rows on top of the blanket. Made out of cardboards about the length of a reading book. Embellished with designs topped with glitter.

Noticing Tanya's interest in his cards. After looking her over for a quick second. The young man turned on his charms. "How you doing miss? You see something you like?"

"Yeah I like all of them. Their very creative. You made all these?"

"Yup, and I have all kinds too. If for some reason I don't though. I can make one right here on the spot."

"What I'm looking for is a birthday card. Which ones are those and how much?"

Stepping over and waiving his hand across the whole third row. He said, "This row right here is all birthday cards. Everything's for ten dollars. Four for thirty if you buy four. If you want one made right now. I usually charge fifteen for that. But since you so pretty I'll bless you for the regular price. Ya heard?…If you don't mind me asking, who's the card for?"

"A friend of mine." "Male or female?" "Male."

Grabbing two cards from out the row. He handed them to her saying, "Check these two out and tell me which one you like. If you don't like either. Remember I can make one for you. It's still the same price and it'll only take about fifteen maybe twenty minutes."

Looking the cards over thoroughly. She found it hard to make a decision. Being as though they were both well made. Favoring the one in her left hand she said, "I want this one."

Taking the other one and placing it back in the row. The man grabbed up a specially made envelope for the cars. Then gave it to her saying, "Yeah that's a good choice. I like that one better myself."

Reaching in her bra, she pulled out a stack of money. Peeled off a ten and handed to him. "Thank You. Stay on your grind and you'll be buying out Hallmark before you know it.", she said with a smile.

Laughing he said, "My thoughts exactly. I appreciate your business. Send some of your friends my way and next time the cards on me."

Stuffing the money back in her bra. Before turning to leave she said flirtatious, "I like hustlas."

Looking her up and down once again he replied, "Yeah I see that."

Giggling, she strutted back down the sidewalk. Putting an extra twitch in her hips because she knew he was watching.

Pulling the 745 into a parking spot out front of some apartments. That were located in the Strawberry Mansion section of North Philly. She hopped out the sports car with card and jewelry in hand. Then walked down the sidewalk to the apartments she was headed to. Climbing the steps leading to the front door. Pressing one of two buzzers labeled Hayes.

After waiting five minutes. The door was opened by a tall, light skin man with out stretched arms. Looking up at him with a smile. Tanya walked into his embrace. "Happy Birthday Greg."

Almost everyday since their tryst at the Adams Mark Hotel in July. They had found time to spend with each other. Whether it be for lunch or a few hours after work. Leaving the only abandoned element of their renewed relationship. The secretiveness concerning each other.

Looking down at the jewelry bag as they disengaged. Greg said, "Now you know you ain't have to get me nothing. Your presence is good enough." "Yeah I know, but I still had to though. It ain't nothing really. Just a little something." She said handing him the bag.

Taking it, he turned and led her inside. Shutting the door behind him before heading to his apartment upstairs. Walking inside his modestly furnished two bedroom asking, "You want something to drink?"

Closing the door she answered with a smile. "That's what I should be asking you. Today is your day. So let me be at your service for the short amount of time we have together. Just sit back, relax, and open your present. I'll be right back."

Doing as he was told he took a seat on the nearest couch. Going inside the bag to check out his gift. While Tanya buried herself at his apartment's minibar. Mixing a drink that she knew he loved with the expertise of a bartender. Coming back in the room holding a black plastic squarish tray laden with a bottle of Hennessey, Coke, and glasses. Taking a seat beside him and slipping off her sandals. After placing his drink in front of him. She curled one leg up and underneath her asking, "So how you like it?"

Seeing the price tag on the gold chain labeled at eight hundred dollars. Made him intensely upset and jealous. The way he always felt whenever she cam around with expensive accessories. Leaving him feeling second rate. Feeling as though he couldn't compete with Telly. Who lavished Tanya so much that eight hundred dollars was "just a little something." Yet he hid the way he truly felt.

"I love it boo. Still though, like I said. Your presence is enough."

"I'm glad you like it. How about that card?"

"Oh, its off the chain. Where did you get it from?", he said, taking a sip of the drink she made.

"From this youngbull up on Erie Avenue. Ima do business with him all the time. I've never seen any cards like that before."

"So, how much time we got to enjoy each other's company?"

Looking at her Cartier watch on her left wrist she said, "About three maybe four hours. I took half a day today. And I got to be home before Tanya gets out of her little program she in."

Drinking up the remainder of his drink. He mixed another one and downed it in one gulp.

Then turned his attention to Tanya's pretty pedicured feet. Directing her to place them in his lap. So he could massage them to both their satisfaction. Until he met the needs of his inner foot fetish. Which was perfectly alright with Tanya. Sipping on her drink leaning back on his sofa. Enjoying his attentiveness.

Then suddenly without warning he got to his knees on the carpeted floor. Sticking his head up under her skirt. Placing his mouth and tongue between her shapely legs. Licking the pussy lips of her panty-less pussy. As she widened her legs to allow him more access. Putting her empty glass on the table beside her. As he slid his tongue inside causing her to grip the back of his head. Twirling her pussy around on his tongue. Moaning with the utmost pleasure...

"Mmmm...Mmmm...Ooooo", she moaned softly.

For the next three hours. They pleasured each other all over the apartment. The living room, kitchen, on top of the minibar, inside the bedroom. Now lying inside the latter naked on top of the sheets exhausted. Greg watched Tanya's perfect figure as she headed towards the bathroom. In order to take a shower before her departure.

Turning around at the doorway. Tanya grabbed both her breasts asking, "You sure you don't want to take a shower with me birthday boy?"

Smiling he said, "Naw, I'll take one later. You wore me out."

Laughing, she headed into the bathroom. Leaving him alone atop of the sheets. Listening patiently for the telltale signs of her securely in the shower. Then once he heard the water fully running, he quickly hopped up throwing on some jeans and sneakers. Rushing out the bedroom towards the minibar where she left her car keys. Grabbed them up with a pen. Then raced outside to the B.M.W.

Shirtless he climbed inside rummaging through the glove compartment. Until he found the title for the vehicle. Then methodically he wrote down Telly's full name and address. Before placing everything back the way he found it. Running back inside to take back his spot in bed. Pretending like he'd been there all along.

He loved her and she loved him. Everything was fine until her baby father came home. Messing up a relationship that was years in the making. He was tired of playing second fiddle. Knowing with his twenty-seven thousand dollar salary a year. As a mailroom clerk for a textile company. He'd never be able to compete with Telly. Nor would he ever be able to bond. They way two people did after making a child. So he'd come to the conclusion that Telly had to go. The sooner the better.

Still hearing the shower fully running. Showing no sign of letting up anytime soon. He leaned over and grabbed the phone on a nightstand. Pressed the button to call the operator. Then slowly said upon getting an answer. "Hello operator. Could you give me the number to the local F.B.I. office?"

Part

3

Chapter 13

Sitting in a beige colored ergonomic swivel chair situated behind a huge oak wood desk. Broke sat in the study of his condo located in Center City on the top floor of a high-rise condominium complex. Checking over some paperwork concerning the many businesses he owned. Double checking his accountant work. Keeping with his motto to "never trust anyone completely." Especially when it came down to money.

This was from where he managed his legitimate business from. His office space being the room he was currently in. Where he kept all the master records dealing with his businesses. —Employees information, bank deposits receipts, etc. The records concerning the illegal money laundered were kept in a much safer place. Other than the place he laid his head at. Constantly being updated and maintained as time permitted. When he made his rounds of his small empire.

Punching away on a calculator while poring over his financial reports. Broke worked nonstop for hours with the drive commonly seen in successful people. Oblivious to everything except the task at hand. Until everything in those documents were checked. Then, laying the papers into a neat pile on the right side of the desk. He got up from where he was seated and walked out the room. Towards a double glass sliding door. That led out onto a wide balcony overlooking the city.

Stepping out underneath the hot sun rays. He looked at the commanding view. Cars and people looking like ants from his vantage point on the sixteenth floor. Slowly a smile started to play across his face. The way it always did when he stopped to think on his accomplishments. He had been broke a lot longer than he was rich. So, even though he'd been in luxury for years now. He still got a certain kind of rush. Ehen just doing something as simple as what he was doing now.

Hearing the telephone ring from behind. He turned to go answer it. Picking up on the fourth ring he said, "Yeah."

"Hello ah Mr. Anderson. This is Danny from the front lobby. You have some friends here to see you. Is it okay to send them up?"

Appreciative of the lobby man's professionalism. Never allowing anyone in that didn't live there. Unless he had permission from the person they came to see. Broke said, "Yeah thanks Dom. It's okay to send them up."

"Alright Mr. Anderson. You have a nice day."

"You too.", Broke said hanging up.

Glancing at the platinum clock on the living room wall. Broke chided himself from his absent mindness. He was so caught up in double checking his financial reports. The block party he was throwing for his old neighborhood. Had completely slipped his mind. Which was highly unusual. Being as though he took great pride in events like these. Just one of his ways of giving back to the community. Providing enormous amounts of food and alcohol. So, families could get together and have a good time.

Heading upstairs to his bedroom to change clothes. He took off what he had on. Then switched into his typical uniform. An all-black dickie suit with some tan Timberland boots on. Grabbed his roll of money off the dresser. As well as his black rubber grip .45 handgun. Then placed them on his person. Then grabbed two bottles of red syrup with a loud laugh. Drinking them both down quickly. Knowing why he was getting a little forgetful these days.

Just as he started to walk back downstairs. The buzzer to his condo sounded. Taking his time, he walked with caution. Even though he knew who came to get him. He still made a point to look through the peephole. Having moved on enemies in the past the same way.

Opening the door, he came face to face with Telly and Animal. "What's up family?", he said shaking both their hands. While closing his door behind him.

"Dat muthafuckin block party, that's what. This will be the first joint I been to in ten years.", Telly said smiling.

Animal and Broke laughed at the look on his face. Heading towards the elevator waiting propped open with a trash can. Telly asked, "Ayo, why that white dude always acting like he don't know nobody? We done been here to see you. I don't know how many times. Dude be having me ready to smash his ass. With that "let me see if he's available shit."

Animal already knew the reason behind it. Being around when Broke first moved in the building. So Broke directed his answer to Telly. "He do that because that's his job. And it's something a nigga like me really appreciate. If for some reason I get a buzz at my door unannounced. Then automatically I'm spraying shit. Word up! Because that tells me whoever at my door. Done crept in this muthafucka. You feel me?"

Seeing the logic in what he said. Telly nodded his head in understanding. As Animal moved the trash can between the doors. Allowing them all entry inside.

Blocks away and the music could be heard clearly. Even though the rolled-up windows of the Chevy Suburban. That Telly, Broke, and Animal were in. Looking for a spot to park amongst the many vehicles. That were parked up and down both sides of the street. As well as some up on the pavement.

"Damn, everybody up in here", Telly said

"It's like this every year too. They know how we do. Wait till you see all the food and alcohol we got. I mean not just no cheap shit. We got Dom P., Moet, Hennessey. You name it fam and its out there. Free of charge, "Animal remarked while scanning for a spot to park.

Pointing over to a spot on a side street. Broke said, "there go a spot right there yo. Fuck it. Just put this shit on the pavement. We'd be forever looking for a spot. Making a right Animal headed towards the spot. While Telly took the time to check his weapon. Releasing his magazine on his 9mm, checking the rounds, the jamming it back in, jacking a round off in the chamber. Knowing his job was gonna be heavy today. Watching the crowds for any enemy. Even though the Broadie Boyz would be out in force.

Hopping the curb in his truck. Animal parked and killed the engine. Pausing briefly to flick his safety off his weapon before getting out. Followed by Telly and Broke doing the same on the other side. Where a crackhead was slowly walking towards them. Both hands in pocket as he came. Foul body odor reaching the men before he did.

"Any of ya'll want to buy a watch. Fourteen K. I swear to God", the man said pulling a watch out one of his pockets.

As soon as he got within arms reach. Showing no signs of stopping. Already keyed up and hyper alert for any threat. Telly suddenly reached out and mushed the man in his face. Sending him falling to the ground with watch and all.

"Hey man, what's the deal?". He said from his position on the ground.

"You too fucking close that's the deal. Don't nobody want to buy that shit.", Telly said towering over him. "Now get the fuck out of here."

Clearly scared, the man got up and ran the other way.

Saying nothing Broke made sure his door was locked. Then side by side they headed in the direction of the music. Stepping around the yellow horses, blocking the street off from traffic. Coming up on the edge of the big crowd. Where different families sat in front of their homes. Laughing and talking amongst themselves. Most recognizing Broke and Animal as they walked past in the street.

"What's up Broke?!"

"How you doing baby? You done got so big."

"Animal what up my nigga!"

Twenty-Second and Ridge Avenue. This was the block Broke was born and raised on. Official ghetto celebrity status he just nodded in greeting. Navigating through the crowd of people dancing in the streets. Dressed in their latest summer attire. Down to the section he had exclusively reserved for the Broadie Boyz. Just alittle ways off from the D.J. table. Where most of the drinks and food was situated at. Near his mothers house who still lived on this block.

As Broke and Animal walked up his mothers steps into the house. Telly stayed outside with members of the Broadie Boyz. Feeling alittle less tension being around his people. Knowing now he had help in doing his job. Comin through the crowded street to where he stood now. Telly had been on pins and needles. "Telly what's good fam?", Petey said shaking his hand.

Looking at Snuff flipping steaks on the grill. Telly responded, "Them steaks that's what. Where the liquor at?", he said glancing around. Then screaming over to Snuff he asked, "Ayo Snuff them steaks about ready?!"

Laughing Petey said, "Goddamn nigga, slow down. You just got here. And already you trying to eat and drink everything up. You home now fam. Trust me we ain't gonna run out of food before you get to the chow line. Besides you got to pace yourself."

Laughing because the shit was funny. Telly took a seat in an empty chair. "Man, fuck you nigga. I miss your silly ass. How's things poppin for you out West? I been heaving good things."

"Shit all good. Holding it down you know how I do. A few renegades I be having to deal with. You know how that goes though. All in a days work", he said taking a pull from a blunt he held.

Inside Broke was going his aunt's kisses. While shaking his uncle's hands. Working his way through the crowded home into the room his mom was in. Closely followed by Animal doing the same thing. Being as though he was basically like family.

Seeing his mom sitting in a chair. Talking to her next door neighbor. Broke stole a kiss from her before she saw him. "Hey ma? Hi miss Jackie."

Looking up his mothers still beautiful face lit up. "Hey Clyde. When you get here?"

"Just a few seconds ago. And I came right in to see you."

"Where my sugar at?", Miss Jackie asked with a frown.

Smiling, Broke leaned over and kissed her too. Just as Animal came walking in. "Hey Miss. Valerie, Miss Jackie", he said coming over to kiss them as well. Checking out the contents of the room. Broke saw it was pretty much the same since younger years. The only thing looking new and out of place. Was the furniture that his mom had let him buy her. "When you gonna let me move you up out of here? Somewhere hot all season round."

"Boy you know you better than that. I don't care how much money you got. I'm staying right here with my friends. I'm too old to be making new friends.", his mother said.

"Now that's real, Animal said while taking a seat.

Taking a seat beside him as everyone laughed. Broke engaged in conversation with his mom. Inquiring about her well being the way sons did worldwide. Then after about an hours talk. He excused himself and headed to his old room. Which was in the basement of the house. Still looking almost the same. Even with the excess stuff his mom stored down their now.

Walking towards a weight bench up against the wall at the farthest end of the room. He placed his pistol on the torn leather seat and sat down beside it. Immediately checking out the pictures plastered on the wall. Of him and friends when he was considerably younger. Each picture bringing back memories crystal clear as he focused. Although none more clearly than the biggest photo on the wall.

Staring at the picture of his only brother. As if in a time machine, he began to drift back. Back down memory lane to his most fondest memory, Back before his brother has been convicted of a triple murder and placed on death row. Back to their dreams together.

........It was summer of "1995". West Coast and East Coast rappers were beefing on wax. It was a time for rivalry. A time for power moves. And him and his older brother Jacob were sitting in a stolen Doge Dynasty. Parked on a back street near Cecil B. Moore in North Philly. Passing a blunt back and forth. Waiting for one of the biggest drug dealers in Philly. To come and visit a girl he was seeing. Who stayed in an apartment building. Only a couple of feet away from where they were parked. A hour passed, then two. Then suddenly, just as they expected Lamar came through, In a midnight blue, four door, 600 Mercedes Benz. Pulling up in front of the apartment building the girl stayed in. Flicking on his hazards as he stepped out into the street. Staring up at one of the buildings many windows.

As he stood staring, everything seemed to come to a stand still. The kind of brief pause that happens in every hood. Whenever a ghetto star comes through. All eyes were on him. Dressed down in a blue Versace shirt with black pants, and matching Stacy Adams shoes. Iced out Rolex on his left wrist. Shining the reflection of the streetlights over head.

Putting his jeweled fingers around his mouth. He screamed in the direction of the window. "Yo Sharon!"

She was a woman he'd been dating for a couple of months. Right now they were getting ready to go out.

Sliding her living room window up. She poked her head out to see who was calling. Looking down she said, "I'll be right down Lamar. Just give me five minutes."

Shaking his head he said, "It never fails."

"Shut up!", she said playfully. "Ima be quick watch." Then she ducked back out of sight and closed the window. Smiling, he went to climb back in the car. As he was in the process of shutting the door. Suddenly, the sound of gunfire echoed in the air. BRAAAAT!! BRAAT!! That's the last sound he heard. As his torn body fell forcefully across the passenger seat. Leaving chunks of flesh splattered on the windshield. Dripping blood down on the dashboard.

"Next time, pay your taxes nigga!", a young Broke with Mac in hand screamed at his dead body.

Then with a loud screech of tires. As suddenly as it appeared. Just like that the car carrying them was gone...

Broke smiled at the remembrance. This was the formation and beginning of the Broadie Boyz. Just two brothers out to make a power move. Lamar was their first target. Being as though he was one of the biggest dealers around. They figured they might as well start at the top. He refused to meet their demands. So they made him the first of their examples. Many more followed afterwards until niggas got the point.

Later they added a childhood friend named Animal. When Jacob got knocked for a triple homicide. Animal and Broke blew up the organization into enormous proportions. Turning the two brothers dreams into reality. Recruiting members from spots as far away as West Philly. Becoming the juggernaut, they were today.

Hours later people were still partying under the streetlights. The Broadie Boyz were scattered all around the block having a good time. Animal was standing a feet from Broke talking to a woman. Broke had a woman sitting on his lap sharing a bottle of Dom P. with him. Telly was sitting within earshot of Broke. Polishing off another plate of food. Washing it down with a fifth of Hennessey. Watching a dice game take place down by the corner store.

Walking over to where Telly sat on the stoop. Snuff called out. "Damn nigga. Your stomach is bottomless. You still eating?"

Mouth full of food Telly said, "Hell yeah. That's what its for ain't it. And I'm taking a doggie bag too. My shorty might want to bust a grub."

"You greedy yo. But you make me feel bad. Because I forgot all about my shorty. She might want something too."

Shaking a half eaten fried chicken leg at Snuff. Telly said, "See that. Ah, see that. That's what wrong with the youth today. So inconsiderate."

Smiling Snuff said, "Cut it out man. You buggin. I'm a responsible mom. I take good care of my wifey and now my newborn."

"A newborn? I ain't know that fam. Congratulations", Telly said with a look of surprise.

"Thanks yo."

"A boy or a girl?"

"A girl."

"Word up! I can definitely relate. I got a daughter that's ten. My pride and joy. One of the best things that ever happened to me."

Nodding his head in agreement. Snuff said, "True dat. I never knew anybody could love like that. Got me thinking about a lot of things. On the real yo."

"Yeah it'll definitely do that."

"Got me thinking about going all the way legit. I done made tons on money. Just peeping the mistakes of others in the past. I know this shit ain't no cross-country run. More like a sprint. Na mean?", he said pausing to look at Broke. "I done already hollered at Broke and everything. He said its all good too. I done paid my dues. Broke's a good nigga too yo."

Thinking about he was living at the moment. Telly said, "Yeah, no doubt. So when you ghost?"

"I don't know exactly yet. But Broke said he'll let me know. Boy I plan on spending mad time with my wifey and daughter. Thinking about marriage too, Fuck it, na mean? We been together forever yo."

"Dats big my nigga. Don't be trying to plant no seeds this way though. Keep that ball and chain shit to yourself.", Telly said laughing. "Sike naw, I'm just fucking with you. Between me and you. I been thinking about marriage too. Same scenario like you. We been together forever."

About to say something but getting distracted. Snuff turned his attention towards the dice game at the corner store. As well as everyone in the nearest vicinity. Upon hearing raised voices coming from the crowd. "That's burnt money yo! You fucked up!", Petey yelled to the man directly in front of him.

Looking at the fist full of money in Petey's hand. The man yelled, "What you mean burnt money?! I ain't crap out! Put my shit back on the ground!"

"This my shit now!", Petey said holding the fist of money at eye level. "You rolled the dice and hit your point! Then instead of picking up your money, you rolled again! That's burnt money!"

"C'mon man! Burnt money?! I ain't never heard of no shit like that in my life! The name of the game is craps! Therefore, if I don't crap out, it don't matter how many times I hit my number then roll again! I don't lose nothing unless I crap out! "Look gang, I ain't gonna keep repeating myself, "Petey said stuffing the money in his pants pocket.

Looking Petey up and down. The man said with a grimace. " I ain't no sucka yo."

At that the man swung off with a two-piece combination. Catching Petey with two hard hooks to the jaw. Knocking Petey against the corner store window. Then he followed up with an uppercut and left hook equally hard. Sending Petey to the concrete conscious, but badly dazed.

That's when in front of that store pandemonium broke out. The nearest Broadie Boyz swarmed the man. Who was now joined by two of his homeboys. They held the rush off as long as they could. Then took off running seeing they couldn't possibly win. As by the seconds more Broadie Boyz joined in.

Shaking it off, Petey hopped up. Giving chase with the rest. As the three men wisely split up. Predictably he was after the man who stole him. Gaining on the crowd in a few seconds. Then passing them in another short few. Sprinting after the man he wanted. Who was now cutting through an alleyway. Slamming trash can behind him. In order to thwart pursuers.

Being the only one after him. While the others chased the rest. Petey jumped the trash cans as they fell. In no time closing the distance between them. To a point where he just dived for the man's legs. Tackling him down on the trash slick alleyway. Both men sliding a few feet across the grime.

As the man spun around on his back. Petey saw a glint of metal in his hands. Instinctively turning the man's wrist away from his body. BOOM! BOOM! Shots from the man's gun ricochet wildly off the brick walls. Concentrating on the gun. Petey made a grab for it. Successfully wrenching it out the man's hand. The victory was short lived though. When the man swung one of his signature hooks. Knocking Petey off him and to the side. Causing the gun to slide off somewhere in the darkness. As he jumped to his feet looking wildly in the darkness. Giving Petey time to pull his gun out his boot. Aiming it while getting to his feet.

Seeing Petey's pistol the man attempted a lunge for it. Although he was brought up short from a smack delivered by the gun.

Stumbling to the side holding his now bleeding head. The man said, "I knew ya'll niggas was pussy. Ain't shit without a gun. I ain't no sucka. I give it to you however. Go ahead nigga, squeeze the trigger."

About to do as he said. Suddenly Petey stopped himself. "Nigga you ain't shit. Anybody can steal somebody." Stepping over to the side a little Petey continued, "I tell you what nigga. Ima sit this gun down right over here. And we gonna go head up. If you come out on top. You know what to do."

In a state of disbelief. The man stared real hard in Petey's eyes. Not believing what he was hearing. As any same man would. Seeing he was serious the man smiled. He was one of the most hard hitting niggas around his way. He couldn't believe his lick. As he watched Petey place the gun well out of reach. "Lights out bitch", he said advancing to Petey.

What he couldn't have known, but found out shortly. Petey was golden gloves. Landing hard blows to his body and face. With the precision of a person trained. In no time sending him stretched out on the ground. Trying his best to remain conscious. As Petey walked over with his retrieved gun standing over top of him.

"Naw nigga, lights out to you clown", Petey said right before emptying out his .38 special.

Cocking his head to the sounds of police sirens nearby. Knowing the commotion at the corner store was probably the cause of their appearance. Petey knew better than to go back to the block party. Hurrying back out the mouth of the alley. He ran towards his car parked on one of the side streets.

Chapter 14

Three weeks after the block party. On a corner of North Philly standing amongst a crowd. Just alittle ways from one of his stash houses. Underneath the September sun. Broke had his back against a wall. Counting money from a rubberband stack in his hand. Watching as Animal prepared his pitbull Sasha for battle. Against another man's bitch pitbull growling by its master. Eager to engage in what it did best.

Both dogs were Grand Champions. Having won five or more matches in the past. So the audience was unusually big. Everybody excited about the coming bout. Like it was a Mike Tyson fight or something. Placing bets on the dogs they favored the most. The majority going with Animal's opponent because of its bloodline. Letting nothing deter it of its objective. When it was on the attack.

Smiling, Broke yelled to the crowd. "I'm taking all bets! I'll even lay odds two to one! To anybody who got a grand or better! Ante up ya'll! Work together! I need that dough!"

Eyes lighting up around the crowd. Several people came over and made a wager with him. Laying money down on the concrete underneath their feet. Feeling like they had a winner. Especially when Animal's opponent started rubbing powder cocaine across his dogs nose. Causing it to growl louder and fierce. Watching the dogs antics. Telly said to Broke in a low voice. "Man, I don't know fam. That nigga dog look shell. Straight up berserko. Got me tempted myself to take the odds you giving. But I know you better than that though. You know something."

With a smirk Broke turned towards Telly in a conspirator way. "You right, a little something. The first thing is, Animal is a dog guru. He know what the fuck he doing. Muthafucka be breeding them pitbulls like a God yo. Word up." Stopping to look at the people nearest him. Making sure they couldn't eavesdrop on his conversation Broke said, "See check it out. Now there's no doubt the other pitbull is from a superior breed. His breed just ain't better than Sasha's. That bitch bloodline is Bolio. They characteristically intelligent dogs. See how collected she is. Just watching that mad beast across from her."

"Yeah, I noticed that. I aint seen a whole lot of dog fights. But the ones I did. Before battle both their dogs was amped."

"Exactly. Now another thing I want you to peep. Is the size of the other dogs head. See how big it is? Makes an easier target. Now see how narrow headed Sasha's is? That's the head of the best bitters. Watch what I tell you fam. Sasha gonna wreck that shit. She might get a little banged up. But she ain't gonna lose though. Trust me."

Waving his hand for the crowd to spread out. Animal began taking the leash off Sasha. Arms still wrapped around her neck. "Watch him girl, watch him, watch", he whispered in the bitch's ears. Getting a little louder he said, "Kill...kill...kill...sic."

Both men stepping back from their dogs. Sent the pitbulls racing towards each other. Sasha coming in high as her opponent came in low. Going directly for the dog's larger head. Sasha bit down on it. While the other dog snapped her jaws towards her neck. Missing it by a half inch. As Sasha dodge out the way. Pulling a chunk off her head with her.

Keeping with the notoriety of his bloodline. The dog immediately rushed again biting Sasha on the side. Tearing flesh as Sasha twirled away again. So fast and preciously done. That for a second the other dog was at a disadvantage.

Facing sideways to her. Which was all the time Sasha needed. In order to bit down on its larger head again. This time gaining the lock it was after the first time. Shaking its head viciously, slamming the other dog to the ground.

"That's right girl. No mercy. Slump her", Animal encouraged.

"Get that bitch off you!", the owner of the dog screamed.

Following its master's command. The dog tried its best. Biting small areas on Sasha's front. Causing Sasha to loosen her lock and dodge alittle. In order to clamp down on her opponents neck. Shaking violently until it was plain to all spectators. The dog with the Red Boy bloodline was no more good.

Looking like he was heartbroken. Watching all the blood pour from his dog's neck. The man called out to Animal in a panic. "Aiight yo. You won. Call her off. You won."

Nodding his head, Animal yelled in a commanding voice. "That's enough Sasha!" Then made a kissing sound with his lips.

Showing how well she was trained. The bitch slowly backing away from the wounded pitbull. Blood dripping from her muscular jaw. Growling out a warning as she did. Until she was beside hr master. Who was busy petting her and checking her wounds. That she sustained in the fight. "Good girl...Good Sasha", Animal whispered soothingly.

Scooping up all the money off the ground. Once he had it all in hand, Broke smiled towards Telly. As they walked back towards the stash house.

"I love dogs yo.", Broke said slipping a thick rubber band around the stacks of bills.

Looking at all the money in his hands. In a humorous way Telly said, "Yeah I know you do."

Stuffing the knot in his pants pocket. Broke said seriously, "Naw fam, I'm not saying that because of the money I just made. I'm saying that sincerely. Niggas could learn a lot from dogs. They the most loyal muthafucka's around."

"Yeah I agree to a certain point though. I say that because you got some pussy ass dogs too. Only thorough breeds be holding it down."

Nodding his head in agreement he said, "True dat, true dat. That's why you got to weed muthafucka's like that out. Get rid of they ass the first opportunity. Because in the long run, they not gonna be no good to nobody. Including themselves. Shit, in fact the thorough breeds will weed the weak out for you sometimes."

Going silent for a second. As Animal came up with Sasha in tow. Both men watched Animal's concern for the dog. Kneeling down beside her. Reaching in a little bad he carried. That held everything he needed to dress her wounds. Pulling out a bottle of peroxide to pour over her bite marks. That was left by the other bitch she just fought.

"That's beautiful right there yo. That's what I mean. When I say niggas could learn a lot. See she know who be holding her down. So she play her position and do as he says. Till the death unconditionally. She wont even let nobody touch her but him. Will try to bite the shit out of anyone who try."

Not really being too much into dogs. Listening to Broke's insight gave him a new appreciation. "That's deep."

Fixing his attention on Snuff smoking a blunt. Then turning back towards Telly, Broke said, "See loyalty and love is earned. Na mean? Can't get it no other way." Pausing for a second he watched Sasha lick Animals hand. "Don't forget about tonight yo."

Watching the dog too Telly said, "My bad, what?"

"I said don't forget about tonight. I know you probably wouldn't forget. I'm just reminding everybody. All the Broadie Boyz gonna be there. So, you'll get a chance to see everybody."

"Oh, I wouldn't miss Snuff's send off for nothing. I'm there."

Driving his B.M.W. for a change. Instead of a car owned by the Broadie Boyz. Telly puffed on a blunt as he navigated through a suburban neighborhood. Out in the Mt. Airy section of Philly where homes were comfortably spaced apart. Looking for the address that Broke gave him. To the send off that was planned for Snuff tonight.

Seeing luxury cars parked up and down both sides of the street up ahead. Telly stopped paying attention to the address. Knowing up ahead was his destination. Finding it hard to believe. That residents up the way kitted their cars down in fancy rims. Or drove anything as outlandish as a Hummer with dark tinted windows.

Pulling up in front of the home. He recognized some of the faces walking down a pathway. Up towards the front entrance of the huge two story home. Another stash house for the Broadie Boyz. Looking for a parking space. He found one a short ways off, parallel parked inside the place, then hoped out walking backwards the entrance he'd seen other people going. Checking out the expensive cars as he passed them. For the first time getting a real sense of the Broadie Boy manpower.

Walking inside, the people nearest the door looked his way. Not recognizing their faces Telly, just nodded. Making his way through the crowd. Looking for a familiar face. Puzzled in his mind as he glanced around. Noticing how it didn't seem much of a send off. There was no liquor, women, or food as far as he could see. He expected a party like atmosphere. Something probably celebrating all Snuff's contributions to the organization.

"Yo Telly! Telly!", Petey yelled from across the room.

Finding the direction, the voice came from. Telly located Petey and walked over. "What's up yo. I thought this was a sendoff. Where Broke and them at?"

"That's what they say it is.", Petey responded. "Broke and them over there with Lacey."

"You ever seen something like this before?"

"Never.", Petey said shaking his head. Then again Sniff ain't your average cat. He been putting in work before Broadie Boyz got so large."

"How long you been here?", Telly asked.

"I was one of the first to arrive. Niggas been gathering for about two hours. Things should be getting ready to get underway. In a little while."

Telly's instinct told him something was wrong. But he couldn't pinpoint the urge. Looking around the room, Telly checked out the crowd. Men were standing everywhere in conversation. Then at that precise moment from across the room, the sound of someone clearing their throat could be heard. Then, Broke stood up from where he was seated. Motioning for Snuff to follow him. As they walked across the spacious wooden floor of the front room. Towards an area in the center where everyone could see. As they came to a stop, Broke immediately started talking. "What's up family? This meeting we are about to have. Has been a long time coming."

Hearing his voice, everyone got quiet. Turning towards his direction and giving full attention.

"What this is about is a send off for one of my favorites. Which is something I'm not ashamed to say. Who is ready to move on. A person who been down with us, probably much longer than the majority of you have. He one of the few that knew my brother Jacob when he was home. And that's been a long time. How long its been exactly Snuff?"

Smiling a little at all this attention. Snuff said, "About six years fam. Three months before Jacob got knocked on those homicides."

"You remember what we used to say all the time? What we said all the time?"

"What you mean?"

"I mean the slogan we used to say all the time together."

Trying to jog his memory, Snuff looked down at the floor in deep concentration. Trying to recall those days when Jacob was still on the streets. Thinking...slogan...slogan...A little over a minute was all it took. Causing him to smile in remembrance. As clear as day he called them standing together with guns in hand. High off marijuana and syrup screaming at the top of their lungs.

Seeing recognition in Snuff's eyes. Glassy eyed off the two bottles of yellow syrup he dumped earlier. Broke yelled in a loud voice for everyone to hear. "All I got is my gun and us, We'll never part ways till death do us?"

Faster than the eye could see. Suddenly a black .40 caliber was in Broke's hand. Aimed point blank at Snuff's face. Snuff's face didn't even have time to register fright. Before his brains was splattered all over the wooden floor.

As Broke squeezed off one shot between the eyes. Calmly watching as Snuff's body followed his brains. Landing on the floor with a thump and a bounce. Shaking like a leaf on a breezy autumn night.

In no way or form expecting something like that. The whole room was in shocked silence. All eyes riveted on Broke standing with a gun in hand. As if he was a raving lunatic or something. Going off the deep end at a moments notice.

Calmly, but loud enough to be heard Broke said, "He wanted out. So I gave him out. Pay attention ya'll because that's the only way out. Lest ya'll forget! Till death do us! I witnessed everyone of ya'll initiations. And explained to everybody. Ya'll listen to these rap songs and so-called gangster movies. And hear that phrase so much. It don't even mean nothing no more. When I told ya'll that, I meant it. I live by it and my brother live by it. Sitting in death row waiting to die. A sacrifice he made so we could live it up. So you best believe I'm gonna make everybody live by it." Passing for a few second to mad ball the crowd. Afterwards he asked, "Anyone else want out?"

Throughout the crowded room. It was mixed emotions. Some niggas was feeling it. While others were feeling real uncomfortable. Telly falling in the later category. Couldn't take his eyes off Snuff laying there oozing from his head. A young man with a newborn. Looking to enjoy life as a family man.

Maybe years before his prison stint. Telly probably wouldn't have gave a fuck. A family man himself looking to get in and out the game. Suddenly he understood the message attempted by the man he killed upon initiation. Ironically Snuff was the same man that give him the weapon to do it with. That same man was trying to get out the Broadie Boyz...Telly cursed himself for not listening to instinct. Tucking the .40 caliber gun back in his wristband, Broke said, "Meeting adjourned. Somebody clean this shit up."

Chapter 15

Groggy from sleep, Broke climbed out from in between the two beautiful dark complexion women he spent the night with. Stumbling across the thick carpeted floor of his condo. In the direction of his jacuzzi equipped spacious bathroom. Emptying himself of all the champagne he drank the night before. Afterwards, taking a seat on the edge of the jacuzzi tub. Head in hands trying to get his bearing.

A few minutes was all he needed to shake of the sluggish feeling. Looking up through the skylight situated in the ceiling of the bathroom. He wondered what time it was. Seeing the light blue sky through the clear glass of the skylight. So he got up leaving the momentary comfort of the porcelain tub. Then headed into his office space to check the time. Finding out that it was a quarter past five in the morning.

Taking a seat behind the desk. He leaned back in the chair, thinking about last night. When he made an example out of Snuff. Which got him thinking about his brother, and all the aspects of his case. How his sacrifices in the beginning. Now had him in luxury like a king. Acknowledgement of his brother's contributions took away any sympathy he felt for Snuff. Did nigga's think they were better than his brother?

Grabbing a yellow legal pad and ballpoint pen. Broke leaned his elbows on the desk and began to write...

Jacob,

What's up fam?! As you already know I miss you nigga. You cam rest assured I'm out here doing everything possible to get you out. I hollered at the lawyers retained for you. He was telling me the other day. The private investigator that work for his firm. Turned up some into that could possibly get you a new trial for one of them bodies. I'm a check him out in a little while to see what's poppin.

In the meantime, Ima keep holding it down. We doing big things out here. Animal still playing his position. Which should come as no surprise. Staying true to our original dream. I saw mom the other day. She maintaining and in good health. I threw a block party for the old hood a couple of weeks ago. It felt good to do shit like that. Word up! Remember when we hardly had any food to eat? Bumming from the neighbors and shit? You always wanted me to do the asking. Even though mom told you do it. It's funny now when I think about it. Back then, that shit wasn't funny at all. Shit was real.

You know what fam? Sometimes I feel like a dying breed out here. I keep it moving regardless though. You know how that goes. Na mean? I woke up this morning thinking about you. So I decided to drop a few lines. I know how it be in there. Niggas that been down put me up on how important a kite is. Until next time, keep ya head up, Till death do us.

1 Luv,

Broke

Writing the address on an envelope. He put the letter inside and sealed it shut. Leaning back in the chair he was sitting in. He ran his hand across the smooth wood of the desk. Contemplative of the last paragraph he wrote in the letter. Informing his brother how he felt like a "dying breed". He couldn't have expressed himself in better words. That's exactly how he felt holding the reins of the organization.

Everybody wanted to make a quick buck, but few wanted to sacrifice. Yeah, they would sacrifice until they got want they wanted.

Then first chance they got, they wanted to turn their back. Like they got to where they were by themselves. Loyalty was an attribute few people seemed to have nowadays. As far as he was concerned with it. The people in his organization that didn't possess this trait, wouldn't be tolerated.

Sitting on the hood of a Broadie Boyz car. Watching traffic pass down the street. Inhaling big puffs from the roach he held. While exhaling, Telly lit another blunt rolled with it. He was currently in the process of making his rounds. Which entailed handling any problem and laying out strategy. To the people running the day to day activities in the stash houses of the area he oversaw. He usually just touched base with the one star in his area. On this occasion he decided to talk to the soldiers on the ground. Being as though they were having a problem getting a payment.

Passing the blunt to a Captain opposite him, Telly said, "Now let me get this right. Whenever ya'll run up on one of his dope spots. It's never more than two grand inside. And all your attempts at shooting his workers up. Seems not to be bringing him any closer to paying up."

"Yup", Tyreem said, exhaling smoke out of his nostrils. "We beat the shit out one of his workers the other day. And found out that's all his dope spots been told to keep at one time. The rest they get out there as soon as they make it."

"And you can't find him either?"

"Naw, word is he don't even live in Philly. Stay out N.Y.C. somewhere. Just got his cousins holding it down out here. Supplying the coke and shit. They real organized too. Can't seem to get a bead on them niggas. No matter how hard I try."

Getting the blunt back. Telly took several puffs looking at the morning sky. Going over this info in his mind. "I heard they got some business they own. Ya'll ain't never seen them out there either?"

"Niggas ducking us fam. One minute they kicking out no problem. Next minute they vanished. No doubt been planning it all along. Just waiting for the right time."

Passing the blunt back Telly said, "You know what. Fuck that nigga. Ain't like he making a whole bunch of money anyway. It becomes a problem when big fishes in violations. That nigga ain't even a medium fish. You feel me?"

Telly said looking him in the eye, "Don't worry about getting no more money from him. This what I want you to do. Just shut the nigga all the way down. Don't allow him to make no more money in our area. Send the message to his workers. That is real unhealthy to be down with him. Also, all the businesses they supposedly got. Molotor Cocktail. Na mean?"

"Molotor Cocktail? What's that?"

At first surprised that he didn't know. Then recognizing the youth on his face. Telly explained, "It's a firebomb. Get a bunch of empty bottles and some rags. Fill them up with half Kerosene and half gasoline. Dip the rag, lite it, and throw the shit inside his business. When the glass bust, Shit gonna start blazing as the flammable spread out." Then as if an afterthought. "Make sure we ain't no civilians there though. Any nigga's living street life fair game though."

Smiling in wonder at the knowledge he just learned. Tyreem nodded in agreement. Reaching to pass the blunt back to Telly.

Waving his hands Telly said, "Naw I'm straight fam. You go ahead and kill it. I got some more runs to make. I'll get back with you. To see how its coming. Jump shit off tonight aiight."

"Aiight"

"One luv", Telly said hopping down off the car's hood.

As he headed to the driver's side getting in. Tyreem hopped down and headed back into the stash house to brief his soldiers. While Telly pulled the car out of parking and into traffic. Cruising through the blocks with heavy thoughts about the predicament he was in.

Seeing what he saw last night. Telly knew he had to come up with a way out a way out with everything still intact. Meaning his family of two, as well as himself. Knowing firsthand the ruthless nature of Broke and his organization. Understanding that nothing was safer or sacred from his wrath. Having orchestrated and participated in the kidnapping of a child himself. He knew what they were capable of.

Looking at his reflection in the rear-view mirror. Telly shook his head pathetically. Funny how he always seemed to have a strategy. In order to fix a problem the organization was faced with. Now concerning a major problem he had. He couldn't even begin to start.

Grabbing a rolled blunt from off the passenger seat. With the same hand he grabbed a lighter. Sparked it up and began to puff. Steering the car with one hand, deep in thought...Disappearance? It was a possibility. Where would he go? How would he do it? Suddenly his mind visualized last nights scene again. The quality of the weed making every detail vivid.

With no emotions on his face. Even after the proclaimed statement "One of my favorites" Broke calmly with no hesitation blew Snuff's brain out all over the floor. A man who helped build the organization. A man like him with a daughter. A woman he loved so much he was thinking about marriage. A man who simply wanted the best for his family. Dead because of another man's way of thinking.

Anger started to creep in his emotions. As he navigated through the residential street. Who did Broke think he was? Why not just kill Snuff outright instead of making a scene? Then a rational part of his mind started working. Didn't Broke say he "Witnessed every one of ya'll initiation?" Didn't Snuff remember the slogan they used to say? Didn't he tell you what was expected on your first day? If greed wasn't so firmly planted in your mind. Clouding your judgement from the very beginning. You as well as Sniff would have understood.

Emotions still running angry. Although now angry at himself more than anything. Telly deeply inhaled the smoke from the burning blunt.

Trying to ease the tension. Mind still racing every which way for an answer. A strategy to remove himself from this self-inflicted trap.

That was the only important thing at this time. Everything else was really irrelevant. What's done is done. He was trapped and Snuff was dead. Now, what was he going to do? In order to insure he didn't end up the same way...

Chapter 16

It wasn't hard to spot her out of the crowd. Dressed in a black dress with matching shoes. Walking beside an older woman that was holding a baby girl in her arms. Filing inside the church with the rest of the people gathered. Even if she wasn't attired in all black. Anyone who could see, would still find it easy to spot her amongst the throng. Looing as if in a state of shock. Pain etched across her face. Seeming as if she was lost.

It was a big turn out. Almost every star member was there from the Broadie Boyz. Come to pat their respects to the dead. No matter how they felt about the situation. Nothing could tarnish the reputation Snuff built for himself. As a live nigga who would give you the shirt off his back. Nor could anything diminish his contributions to the organization. Therefore he was respected in death as well as life.

Finding a seat in the second pew of the church. Behind the immediate family sitting on the first pew. Right in front of Snuff's closed wooden casket. Telly looked at the framed picture sitting on top of the casket. Comparing the features with the baby girl held in the older woman's arms. Saddened at the fact she would never know her father. Except through the picture the mother held as life went on.

Scanning his eyes further down the first pew. Telly's eyes landed on Broke's face. Sitting next to Animal with his arms crossed. Starring at the picture atop the casket too. Showing no emotions in his face. As the preacher came out to start the service. Stepping to the podium with a worn Bible in hand. Greeting the almost full church in his baritone voice.

Tuning the preachers words out. Telly thought about the course of action he planned on taking. Encouraged even more so by the melancholy mood of the preceding right now. Noticing Snuffs funeral how things could turn out for him. Girlfriend looking lost staring at his closed casket. Daughter growing up to womanhood without him.

Members of the Broadie Boyz coming to pay homage. While the one responsible for his death sat in the front row emotionless. Looking as if this was a more formality. Something being done just because he had to.

The service taking place didn't last long. After all he was a street nigga. The family knowing this full well. Figured he wouldn't want a whole lot of gospel hymns being sung at his funeral. So the only thing they insisted on was a preacher. Giving the proper send off traditional to most people that passed away. Afterwards allowing people to file past the closed casket. Giving their wishes and encouragement for the family seated. As well as getting their last look at Snuffs picture perched on top of the casket.

Following the long line around. Telly was honestly surprised at what he saw. He thought he was probably the only one going to give a gift. Instead, what he saw was every member of the Broadie Boyz. When they passed Snuffs baby mother, handed her cash money as a gift. The pile was getting so big, that they had to bring out a church basket in order to hold it in.

When Tellys turn came, he dropped ten thousand in cash in. Then turned to Snuffs baby mother handing her a slip of paper. "That's my home phone number on there. My name is Telly and if you ever need anything don't hesitate to call. And I mean anything."

Overwhelmed by sorrow and the generosity of everyone, tears flowed down Shawna's check as she muttered. "Thanks Telly."

With a sympathetic smile and a nod, Telly went on his way. Stopping only for a brief second in front of Broke and Animal. "Im gone fam. Back on the job. Na mean? You need me around for anything else?"

"Naw, Im good for today. Animal will be good enough.", Broke answered.

"Aiight.", he said with a nod goodbye.

Walking back down the aisle and out the church. Choosing to forgo Snuffs burial. Telly hopped in a green colored Cherokee Jeep. Then pulled out in traffic headed towards his area of operation and responsibilities. In a certain section of North Philly. Not really too far from where he used to stay down Susquehanna.

Pulling the Jeep in a parking spot across the street from the restaurant he managed. Telly hopped out and went inside. Finding as always, the place packed with customers at noon. Eager to enjoy the well-cooked food provided. That was cooked by a friend of Animal.

"Hey Telly!", a young woman in a conservative suit yelled.

Looking over the crowd for the source. His eyes fell on a regular customer waving her hands in the back. He went to school with her at Benjamin Franklin. Crossing the room he headed to the table. "What's up Lenise?!" Watching closely the expression on his face she asked, "You alright? You don't look like your normal self."

"Im good. I just came from a friends funeral. That's all."

"Im sorry", she said sympathetically.

"It's all good", he said looking at his Rolex. Trying to convey the vibe that he didn't have time at the moment.

Picking his vibe she said, "Well I was just about to leave. I was just checking on you."

"And I appreciate it. See you next time.", he responded politely with a polite nod.

Walking back across the room pass some of the employees waiting tables. He went by them without so much as a word. In the direction of his office situation back behind the kitchen area. Off in the corner behind a heavy steel door.

Reaching it he placed the key in the lock. Then entered inside, shutting and locking the door behind him. Taking a sear in a grayish colored swivel chair. Tat sat in front of a metal desk. Underneath which sat a heavy black fireproof safe. That was built inside the floor.

Staring down as if it was a snake poised to strike him. For a brief moment, Telly hesitated for what he was about to do. Knowing from this moment on, the particular action he planned on taking was irreversible. A path down which one taken, had in no way or form a way to back track.

Leaning down he spun the combination on the safe. Successfully in one try getting the proper selection and opening it wide. Revealing inside almost full safe filled with stacks of money. Broadie Boyz money extorted from his area. Earmarked for laundering through his restaurant on a weekly basis. Being placed in a night deposit box once a week by him. Unbuckling his pants, he reached inside pulling out several stacks. Stuffing them inside the pockets of the cargo pants. That he had on underneath his baggy jeans. Positioning it just right so as not to be noticed. By anyone who may have taken an interest.

He planned on making his exit from the organization. Just as soon as he was ready. In the meantime, he was going to steal as much money as he could in between. In order to insure a most prosperous future for his family. When they made for their escape. Or if anything happened to him before or after such a dat. He wasn't a believer in half stepping. Prison time had showed him the error in that thinking pattern. If one was gonna do something, he should do it in gigantic proportions, or not at all. He planned on doing just that.

Part

4

Chapter 17

Tucking the .45 handgun under the seat out of view. Telly climbed out the white, four door, Nissan Maxima. Heading across the crowded parking lot towards the school entrance. Running up the many stone steps inside the front double doors. So he could make it to his seat before the play got too far along. His daughter Tahira was acting in a play after school. So he made some time between his responsibilities as a Broadie Boy to be here for her performance. Not wanting to disappoint her by not showing. Being as though for the past couple of weeks. Whenever he was home, that was all she talked about.

Navigating the long hallways towards the school auditorium. Quietly he opened the steel door and stepped inside to a fully packed auditorium. Everyone focused in on the performance taking place at the moment. Involving a little white boy and black boy. Walking up and down the stage. In what appeared to be medieval type clothing from circa Rome.

Scanning the crowd Telly looked for Tanya. Who was supposed to meet here in from of the auditorium. Although because he was late, she was now somewhere speckled in the crowd. Consisting of a mixture of white and black families. They stayed out in the suburban section of Chestnut Hill and surrounding areas. Where Telly had brought his home back a couple of months ago.

Finding where Tanya was seated, Telly walked down the ramp aisle of the auditorium. Directly to the seat she saved beside her for him. Located right by the aisle. So when Telly did arrive, he wouldn't have to struggle with his tall frame.

Taking his seat quickly. Telly leaned over and kissed Tanya on the neck. "It took me a little while to get away. Did I miss her performance?", he said in a hushed tone.

"No, you good. It only started about fifteen minutes ago. Her part comes up somewhere in Act two. She supposed to be the wife of a noble."

With a low laugh he imagined his daughter playing that role. "Get the fuck out of here."

Looking his way Tanya whispered, "You ought to know that dummy. As many times as she done told you."

"Shit she talked about that shit so much. I be half listening sometimes." Giving him a funny look Tanya said, "Alright that's enough talk. I'm trying to watch the play."

Turning his lips down as if to say excuse me. Telly got comfortable in his seat and starting paying attention as well. Extremely pleased with the atmosphere his daughter was in. Knowing from experience how much more the curriculum was advanced. Compared to the elementary schools located in the inner city. Where the children hardly even had books. Let alone an acting class as it was at this school.

For about an hour Telly watched the performances. Immensely confused at the little kids doing their thing. Expressing themselves in "art thou's and mayeth thee's." Then suddenly off to the side dressed in what looked like a white robe. Tahira came walking on stage with her head held high. Face situated in the most regal of looks.

Immediately Telly started clapping loudly. Even though Tahira hadn't even said a line yet. Shouldering Tanya as if she couldn't see saying, "There she go. Check out her costume."

Grabbing Telly's hands with an embarrassed look. Tanya said in a low voice, "I see her. You only supposed to clap at the end."

Giving her a look like he would do as he wanted. Telly leaned up in his chair to focus on his daughter. Just as she started her lines. Like the rest with thee's, thou's, and seeth. Her part allowing her to command the stage for about forty-five minutes. Quoting her lines exact and with no mistakes. After which she walked backed off the same way she came in. Regal looking as can be. Causing Telly to stand up and clap enormously loud. Even whistling with delight until she could no longer be seen.

Sliding unnoticeably down in her seat with a red face. As everyone in the vicinity turned their way. But at the same smiling from Telly's silliness. Tanya playfully hit Telly when he sat back down. Bringing laughter from the already smiling faces of people sitting nearest them. Then quietly they sat and watched the remainder of the play. Until it was completely over.

Standing near the stage exit with the rest of the families. Waiting for Tahira to get out her costume and come out. Telly stood quietly up against the wall. As Tanya talked to a black woman she knew nearest her. A few minutes passing by before Tahira came walking out. Holding a small gym bag in hand.

Seeing her, Telly walked over and picked her small frame up in his arms. "Thou wereth thee greateth nobleth wifeth Ieth evereth sceneth", he said playfully.

Giggling and happy to see him. Tahira just beamed her beautiful smile. As he gently placed her back on the floor. Tanya noticing her for the first time said, "You were perfect. Were you scared?"

"Nope, I did that trick you told me to do. So I was alright."

Grabbing Tahira by the hand. Tanya turned back to the woman she was talking to. "Alright Brenda. I'll call you later. And let you know if we can make it to your party."

"Okay then, take care.", the woman called as they started to walk away.

Making it outside going down the school's front steps. Telly asked, "Who was that woman? And what party she talking about?"

"Oh. She stay down on the same block as us. Right in that red colored house across the street near the corner. You know the one with the beautiful hedges.", she said pausing while Telly thought. Then once he shook his head in recognition she continued., "They be throwing parties and what not. We are invited to the next one going down."

"When is it?"

"Next Friday night. You think you can make it?" "I'll see."

Interrupting their conversation Tahira asked, "Daddy can we go eat at that restaurant that serves french food?"

Smiling down at his daughter, Telly looked at his watch. "Later on when I come home. I promise. Right now I need to get back to work."

That's all she needed to hear. As they stopped walking in the middle of the parking lot. Getting ready to part ways. "Aiight ya'll I see you two tonight. Ya'll twoeth beth goodeth", he said giving them both a quick kiss.

Smiling he headed towards the Maxima. As they both laughed behind him.

Speeding down the freeway back towards the inner city. Telly was eager to get back to playing his position. Before anyone started really missing him. Ever since he started stealing money over a month ago, he had to admit his movements were looking kind of erratic. Not showing up where he was supposed to be at consistent times. Compared to how he used to move before.

Anybody paying close enough attention would have noticed. So he tired his best to keep his movements as inconspicuous as possible. Going to his daughters play wasn't helping the cause at all. But he took the risk anyway. After all she was what he was doing everything for.

The reason why his movements were looking erratic was because there were only certain times he could steal money. Without raising any alarms amongst the people in the know of daily operations. Before any of the money made a legitimate business could be placed in a bank night deposit box. It was always counted up by at least two numbers. Being some what of a safeguard from actions such as Telly's right now. A security measure being put in place early in the Broadie Boyz formation.

That's why when Telly was a Captain. He would always count up money with his Superior Lacey, at the bar he was stationed at in West

Philly. Because every night Lacey put the money in a bank deposit box. Fortunately for Telly, concerning his area's set up. The restaurant and Barber Shop he managed wasn't expected to make as much money as Lacey's bar. So he didn't have to deposit the launder money every day. He only had to do it once a week. Giving him ample amount of time to tap the stash throughout the week.

Thinking about what he was doing with the money. Once he got his hand on it. Knowing how much of a risk it was riding around in the car with all that money all day. Telly reached for the cell phone on the passenger seat. Then punched in a few numbers while steering with one hand.

After several rings the phone was answered by a computer. Informing him to hold while music played in the background. After about five minutes a woman's voice answered. "Hello, Mello National Bank. May I help you?"

"Yeah, how you doing? Can I speak to Jonathan Phifer?"

"I'm doing fine sir. May I ask who's calling?"

"Telly Williams"

"Please hold, I'll switch you right over", she said hitting a button.

A few moments later a man's voice spoke, "Johnathan Phifer, Chief Financial Officer. How's it going Telly? How can I help you?"

"What's up Johnathan. I'm just calling to check and see how that trust fund been coming along. The one I have in my daughter's name."

Tapping some keys on the keyboard in front of him. After checking the screen, he said, "Its currently at two-hundred and eighty thousand with a healthy growth rate every month. I invest the interest every month as agreed. In a very diversified way. By the time your daughter turns twenty-one she should be very wealthy."

"That's exactly what I hope. I was just calling to check up on things. I know how volatile the market is. Where things can go haywire from one minute to the next. Leaving the person who only goes by the monthly statement given by the bank. Completely in the dark on certain things."

"Don't worry Telly. I can understand your concern. I get calls everyday from clients wanting to know the same thing. Which is preferably alright. That's apart of my job. Another thing that's apart of my job is that I've been to school and trained to do this. So trust me Telly. You have nothing to worry about."

"Aiight then Johnathan. I'll let you go."

"Have a nice day Telly. And feel free to call me anytime."

Hanging up the phone by pressing a button. Telly tossed the cellphone back on the passenger seat. Feeling real good about how things were going so far. Kinda at peace in his mind. Knowing that if anything happened to him or Tanya, his daughter would be more than alright in the future. With a trust fund account totaling somewhere in the millions.

Hopefully if everything went according to his plan. Nothing would or could happen to either of them. Still steering the car with one hand. Telly reached over to palm the .45 handgun laying it next to the cellphone. Experiencing an immense comfort as he cradled it in his palms.

Chapter 18

Something wasn't right. Even if he hadn't noticed the hard facts in black and white. When he was going over his financial reports. Deep down inside his instinct told him the truth of the matter. Either somebody was having difficulty collecting money. Or somebody was deliberately coming short on dough. Whatever the case may be. There was one thing that Broke was extremely certain of. He was gonna personally get to the bottom of it. And he planned on getting to the bottom of it quickly.

Walking up the stash house steps. Past soldiers sitting around out front. He could tell from the look on their faces. They were completely surprised to see him at the moment. He made his rounds every once in a while. This particular time wasn't one of them though. He usually did it by himself as well.

Followed by Animal inside, Broke scanned around the room for the person he came to see. Finding him sitting in a chair slowly loading up his weapon's magazine. "Tyreem what up yo?"

Looking up from what he was doing. Tyreem was equally surprised by Broke's visit. Laying his weapon down he immediately stood up with outstretched hand. "What's going on Broke? Animal what's good?"

Shaking his hand Broke said, "Just making my rounds." Trying his best to keep the suspicion out his voice. "Let me holler at you in the kitchen."

After shaking Animal's hand, Tyreem led the way back towards the kitchen. Where a few soldiers sat getting blunted. "Ayo, ya'll excuse yalselves for a little while.", Tyreem said to the men.

Seeing who was with him, without saying a word the men got up and left. Nodding in greeting to Broke and Animal, As they passed by into the other room out of earshot. Taking seats in the room where Tyreem was previously.

Taking a seat at the room's lone table Broke asked, "So, how's everything going this way?"

Still standing and leaning up against the sink Tyreem answered, "Everything's doing good Broke. A few resistance we got to get at every now and then. But you know that's always going to be. If a nigga can duck us, he gonna try. The majority make their payment like clockwork though. They know what time it is. Which is fine with me. Makes my job that much easier."

Speaking for the first time, Animal asked, "Offhand, you know how much that be?"

If their unexpected visit was such a surprise to him. The question Animal just asked was even more so. Whenever Broke made his routine rounds. He never asked questions such as that. Such things concerning the money collected was a discussion his superior's had together.

Grateful for his foresight when got promoted. Tyreem answered, "Sure do. I keep a written record of that stuff just in case. You never known when something might happen. I'll go dig it out the stash now."

As Tyreem walked downstairs into the basement. With a pleased look on his face Broke said, "It ain't gonna take long at all." "Yeah you right. I ain't never heard of nobody with his status keeping a record before."

"Yeah, now we got something concrete to compare. Even if he happens to be the one putting shit in the game. I am still cross check that with my record. And figure out what the hell is going on. Shit ain't start slacking out this way. Until a little over a month ago."

"And shit like that just don't happen for no reason. If somebody digging in the stash—-"

Coming back up from the basement. Tyreem held in his hand a black composition book. In which all the figures could be found concerning the money since his promotion to Captain. "This here got all the figures for the past six-months. I mark it down every time we collect."

Reaching over and taking the book from him. Broke stood up from where he was seated. "Aiight Tyreem Ima holla at you. I'll get this book back to you as soon as I can. In the meantime, keep holding records." Pausing for a second, Broke just stared at him. Juggling in his mind what he was about to say next. Figuring correctly that no matter if Tyreem was wrong or right. He would still do what Broke wanted. "Plus, if anybody inquires. This was just a routine visit. Only if anyone asks. You got me?"

Tyreem nodded his head in understanding.

Walking back out the stash house over towards Animal's Suburban Truck. They climbed inside out of the cool fall air. Broke relaxing in the seat. As Animal pulled the truck out into traffic. Steering with one hand while adjusting the knob on his stereo. Turning the volume down lower so he could hear Broke.

"Gaging from lil' homie's reaction back there to our visit, I can tell whatever is going on, he ain't apart of it. If he is, then the nigga deserves an Oscar nomination. I mean ain't no nigga gonna keep a record of every thing and be stealing shit. If he was, these numbers would be in accordance to what he wanted them to be. I done already taken brief glances inside this book. And I can already tell the figures is at way more money than we receiving."

Taking his eyes off the road ahead for a second. Animal glanced over towards Broke who was staring at him. Neither one saying a word. Although both communicating to each other in silence. Exactly the thoughts that crossed their minds. Which was that if it wasn't Tyreem. Then it could only be one other person. Being as though they were the only two who handled the money.

Not trying to be so quick to think ill of Telly. A person that he had come to really like. Animal took on a different avenue of thinking. "I'm saying doe fam. Something don't seem right to me. Check this out! Everything we know about Telly is trill and he ain't no dumb nigga. Them niggas count that dough up together according to procedures.

So why would Telly dig in the stash? Knowing this other nigga know how much dough it is too. And if push come to shove could rat him out...Plus, Telly know how we get down. And he really ain't got no reason to do no shiesty shit like that. We made it possible for him to come from nothing to baller status. Literally fam! You say he ain't even have no clothes right?"

Looking at the situation from this different perspective. Broke nodded his head in agreement. "True dat"

"So it seems to me, a nigga might be trying to make it seem like Telly violating. All the while he the one doing that sneaky shit. Because now that I think about it, that record he keep looks real convenient."

"I see what you saying. Or it could be the other way around too.", Broke said keeping the whole situation in view. "At the moment Ima concentrate on these figures though. This will be the beginning."

Seeing the conversation to be at an end. Animal reached over and turned the radio back up. Thoughts in his mind about the predicament at hand. As he piloted the Suburban through the city streets.

Chapter 19

A week after Broke's visit to his area's stash house. Telly sat in front of the same lone table Broke sat at a week ago. Staring at the wall opposite him. Feeling less tension now than he did earlier in the week. Still a little edgy though from the news he heard from his soldiers. About Broke and Animal coming through on a so called "Routine Round" unexpected. Logically coming to a particular conclusion. That if it was anyway they were on to him stealing. He would already have been dead.

Back when he had first been given command over this area. He had noticed the out of the ordinary habit of Tyreem. In which he kept a personal record of all the money collected. At the time it seemed strange. And he was almost at the point. Where he was going to tell Tyreem to stop doing it. Simply because, if the police for some reason ran up on them. A record of everything would make their job much easier.

Then when everything went down over a month ago concerning the killing of Snuff.

Telly saw a way he could use that habit in his plan. Just in case they caught on to him before it was completed. Thereby creating a situation where they couldn't tell who was doing what. Buying himself some time before they figured it out. Confident by then that would be long gone.

Tyreem had assured him that it was really a routine round. Everybody that was present saying it only lasted a few minutes. Still though, Telly had his doubts. He thought he probably had nothing to worry about. At the same time though, he couldn't afford to just disregard it. He knew he was playing a dangerous game. With that knowledge he acted accordingly regardless.

Walking inside the kitchen where Telly was seated. A recently promoted lieutenant named Larry. Took a seat across the table from him. "Yeah, what's up Telly? They say you wanted to see me."

Taking his focus from off the opposite wall. Telly looked over towards the young man. A guy who had been down with this stash house for a while. Recently promoted a couple of days ago for his outstanding performance. "Yeah that's right. I figured I'd holla at you for a few. And share a few of my experiences on leadership. That could probably make your transition a little easier. I heard you seem to be having difficulty controlling the soldiers on missions. They say you even bumped heads with somebody one time."

"Yeah, niggas be wilding head first and shit. Before the old lieutenant Kareem got knocked. It's true, they always been like that because he let them. I wasn't never feeling that rough. When niggas be out of control. Going above and beyond duty. Things can quickly spiral out of control. Possibly causing every body to get fucked up in some way. Niggas ain't got no discipline! So I be trying to rein them in a little. Not on no dictatorship, but just trying to get them to tighten up a little bit."

"I see what you saying little homie. And you know what, that's exactly how shit should be. If this was a military...." Pausing to lift one finger in the air. Telly said with raised eyebrows. "Yeah we organized in a similar way. But what you have to understand is that these are street niggas. Our strength lies in them being themselves. All you need to do is give instruction and make sure the objective is reached. It don't matter how. As long as the job gets done. If they want to smack a muthafucka with a gun, or bust somebody. Fuck it! Na mean?! Just concentrate on completing the mission and move out. You feel me? You can't make nobody be you. All you can do is give a nigga direction. Point him and then let a dawg be a dawg."

Leaning back in his seat Larry thought on what was being said. Then after about five minutes of silence he said, "Yeah, I think I understand."

"Aiight then. Try it out in alittle while. When ya'll go out and collect that dough. Try to be quick tonight too. So me and Tyreem don't be here mad late counting shit up."

With a nod of his head. Larry got up from the table leaving Telly alone once again. Looking at his watch and seeing the time. Telly yelled in the direction of the other room. "Yo Tyreem! Let's get on the job!"

Hearing Telly, he got up from where he was seated. Taking a last pull on the blunt he was smoking. Before passing it off and heading in the kitchen. "Aiight, I'm ready."

"Yeah go ahead and bring it up. By the time the rest of the dough get here in a few. We should be about finished."

It was that time of the week of the money to be deposited in the bank. So Telly sat eagerly waiting to count the money. Of course his eagerness was attributed to something much more different than the rest of them...

Sitting in the V.I.P. section of the Club "Triple Five". A nightclub he personally owned. To each side of him sitting beautiful women. A different set wanting to be his company tonight. Broke rubbed his hand across the one on his left firm thing. While looking at the one on the right with syrup induced glassy eyes.

"I feel like dancing Broke. Let's dance..", the woman on his right said smiling.

"Go ahead shortie, I'm good. I'll just sit here and watch you shake that pretty ass. You know that's something that turns me on right?"

Standing up, the woman swished her ass alittle for Broke. As she walked into the aisle of the V.I.P. section. Instantly starting to gyrate her hips in rhythm with the music. When she got about ten feet away from Broke's table. Looking like a video girl out on an audition.

Eyes glued on her shaking ass. Broke grabbed the woman seated with him hand. Then placed it on top od his dick. Understanding immediately what he was getting at. She quickly unbuckled his pants. Then proceeded to stroke him up and down. In the shadows of where they were seated.

A few minutes into his freaky sex capade. In no time the woman brought him to a climax. Leaning over to take him between her red colored lips. Slowly sucking him clean. As suddenly just at that moment. Inside his pocket, his pager vibrated.

Reaching inside, he glanced at the number. Placing it back inside, he caressed the woman's hair with her face in his lap. "Aiight luv. Save some for tonight. I got to go make a phone call."

Sucking on him for about four more minutes. Finally she raised her head and began to buckle him back up. Standing up her grabbed for his gun sitting on the table top. Before walking past the woman on the dancefloor with a smile. On out to and exit to the sidewalk towards a payphone located nearby.

Glancing at the number again on the pager. He fished inside the pocket for some change. Slid the correct amount into a slot. Then punched in the numbers. After one ring he was answered on the other line. "Yeah." 'What up Larry?! What you got for me fam?"

Since the uncertainty of who was stealing the money from him. Animal had arranged per Broke's orders. For Larry to be promoted to a lieutenant spot. Not only because he deserved the promotion. But also for the specific purpose of keeping track of the money collected. Reporting to Broke the numbers daily as he knew them.

Holding the payphone receiver between his neck and shoulder. Larry unfolded a piece of paper he held in his hands. "Aiight this what it is for today. Ten grand from them boys right off of Cecil B. Moore. Ten more form them cats down by Richard Allen. And twenty grand form chief down Susquehanna Ave. For a total of forty. Tyreem and Telly counting it up now. As a matter of fact, they should be about finished by now. I had to make a quick run before I could call you."

Mentally memorizing the figures Broke said, "Good job youngbuck. I truly appreciate it. Stay on the D.L. now though. You don't wan to alert this nigga to your presence. You know how a grimey muthafucka be. They don't trust nobody because they know how slimy a person can be. Their reminded everyday when they look in the mirror."

"They ain't on point. I'm playing it cool."

"You ain't told nobody what you up to have you?"

"Naw, because you said not to."

"I'm just double checking you feel me. I'll holla at you next time." About to hang up the phone. Before he did, he stopped bringing the receiver back to his ear. On second thought fam. Just chill for now. I'm good on the figures. I only needed a weeks' worth to get to the bottom of this shit. I'll let you know if I need anymore of your help. Take it easy youngbuck."

"Aiight Broke.", Larry said hanging up his phone.

Hanging up his end. Broke crossed his arms and leaned up against the grayish metal encasing the phone. Scooping the hood on his red Polo hoody onto his head to protect him from the chilly night air. Watching the passengers of cars ride past on their way to get inside his club.

He now had just about all the info he needed. In order to understand who was doing what with his money. All he needed now was to check the record that Tyreem kept. A record that would unerringly point the finger at the culprit. If it was Tyreem then the numbers from Larry wouldn't match his. On the other hand if they did match. Then it would clearly be seen that Telly was the one digging in the stash.

Broke didn't like his kindness being taken for weakness. Throughout his whole career in the streets he never snaked nobody. Yeah he took money, but that was straight up. Wasn't nothing sneaky about jacking niggas. Everybody know who the Broadie Boyz were and what they did. As well as who ran it too.

Balling his fists in anger inside the hoody pockets. Broke turned to walk back inside the club. Thoughts in his mind of the age old saying that "Give a nigga an inch and he'd take a mile."

Chapter 20

Closing the front door to a crack. So as to minimize the noise coming from the party inside Brenda said, "Thanks for coming Tanya. I really enjoyed your company. Feel free to drop by anytime you like. We have a lot in common. Unlike some of those other people inside there." Giggling she looked towards Telly with a sexy look. "And it was nice to meet you. Ya'll don't be strangers." More amused than anything at Brenda's obvious attraction to Telly. Tanya said, "Yeah, we wont. See you later Brenda, and tell your husband I said bye."

"Will do", she promised as they turned to leave.

Walking down the paved driveway. Tanya waited until she heard the door shut. Before bursting out in laughter. Looking at Telly holding her stomach. "That woman couldn't take her eyes off you all night. I wonder if her husband noticed."

"And that's funny? Why you ain't defend my honor? I was expecting you to spazz out and get straight ghetto up in that muthafucka. Busting that bitch in her bead with your shoe and everything.", he said playfully.

"Yeah right. Maybe if I was still in high school. Over the years I've come to like when somebody want something of mine's they can't have. And will never have. Kinda turns me on too."

On the sidewalk now, they walked at a leisurely pace. In no rush to get back to their home at the farthest end of the block. After truly enjoying the social party thrown by their neighbor. Which was a far cry from the type of parties they were used to. Surprisingly though, the new experience was a lot of fun to them.

Wrapping his arms around Tanya's waist in her black Versace dress. Telly said, "See there you go with that freaky shit again." Then turning serious he asked, "You really like this new lifestyle don't you? I mean it goes without saying. That of course you like all glamour you have access to. After being in the slum damn near all your life. What I'm asking is, you like the social environment too don't you?"

Looking up at the full moon in the night sky. Which was beaming down on the quiet suburban streets. Tanya answered, "Yeah, I really do."

Deciding to drop the bomb on her Telly said, "Yeah, I do too. No doubt. And most likely this kind of social setting isn't going to change. The neighborhood might though."

Glancing over his way she asked, "What you mean? You don't like this neighborhood? We haven't even been staying here that long yet."

"I love this neighborhood. The safe environment, school, etc...But there's some circumstances developing that might require us to move. Same social setting, but just a different area.

"Why?", she asked slightly disappointed.

"It's best you don't know. You know how it is. It got to do with them streets. Just trust me."

Knowing how he felt about her getting into his underworld activities. At first she wad content to hold her tongue. Then uncharacteristically, anxiety got the best of her. With a worried look she asked, "Are we in some kind of danger?"

Hearing the worry clearly in her voice. He figured telling her the truth wasn't going to do no good. She might faint on the spot. If he told her "Yeah boo, it's a strong possibility that the most notorious organization in the city shortly would be gunning for him." So he decided to lie saying,

"Naw luv ain't nothing like that. It's just a precaution I'm talking. Just thinking a little ahead. You feel me?"

She didn't answer as they turned into their driveway. Walking past Telly's Beemer on up their front steps and into their home. Plasma screen T.V. showing a movie that wasn't being watched. Greeted them as they closed the door and stepped inside. Stretched across the plush cushioned couch Tahira lay asleep.

Their two storied home was decked out now. An extreme opposite to it's bare insides when Telly first brought his daughter out to see it. It was now equipped with the latest in everything. Customized designer couches. Plasma screen television in the front room with a state of the art sound system. That made it sound like a movie theater when in function. Carpets so soft a person's feet sunk down on them. A fully equipped bar located in between the kitchen and the front room. It even had two six-figure paintings from the sixteenth century adorning the walls.

Grabbing the remote control from off the floor near Tahira. Telly clicked the T.V. off. "Make me a drink baby, and bring it upstairs when your done."

Kicking her black Fendi pumps off her fishnet stockinged feet. She nodded and headed over to the bar. While Telly placed the remote down and headed upstairs to their bedroom. Walking into the adjoining bathroom in front of the marble sink. Gripping the mirrored medicine cabinet above it on both sides. Giving it a jerk upward causing the cabinet to come unhinged. Revealing behind it a wall safe he had installed upon their arrival.

Pushing the cabinet aside on its hinges. Telly turned the combination lock to the correct sequence. Then opened the fireproof door to numerous stacks of money inside. It was so much money inside, it pressed tightly up against the walls. It was barely enough room left for anymore.

Leaving it open he went back into the bedroom. Taking a seat on a black recliner situated by the window. Staring across the street into a neighbors lighted living room. Watching as the old married couple sat watching television.

Shortly he was joined by Tanya. Drinks in one hand, bottle of Hennessey under her arm, and pumps in the other hand. "Here you go.", she said handing him the drinks.

Taking a quick sip Telly said, "You know that safe in the bathroom."

"Yeah"

"Go in there and look inside. Then come back in here so I can holla at you."

Finding his directive kind of strange. She dropped her pumps by the king sized bed. Then walked inside the spacious bathroom. Looking inside the safe. The amount of money inside made her draw a deep breath. She had no idea they had this much money in the house. All the money she needed, Telly just gave it to her. Nor was she really concerned.

As she came back in the room. The look of astonishment was clear on her face. "Check this out! You know that pager I got you a little while ago?", Telly asked.

"Yeah."

"From here on out. I want you to make sure that it's by you all the time. You hear me?" Pausing until she nodded he continued, "Tonight Ima give you a number. That if you when I punch it into your pager. I want you to stop whatever your doing. Get Tahira and the money in the safe. And get missing as quickly as you can. Only take what you can carry. Everything else, fuck it.

Starting to feel uncomfortable from the intensity in his voice, knowing that his talk about a "precaution: was a lie. She asked, "Where to? Where should I go?"

Taking his time pouring another drink. Telly didn't immediately answer. He just guzzled down the glass he just made. Then got up to cross the room. Where a small desk and chair sat in the corner. A spot he sometimes sat at when he was counting up money.

Going inside the top right hand drawer. He puled out a small piece of paper. Crossed the room the Tanya sat on the bed. Gave her the paper, and then took up his previous seat.

"New York City", she said reading the paper he gave her.

"Yeah, stay at the address until I get there."

A whole different city Tanya thought with a questioning look on her face. Suddenly something dawned on her. "What if I don't get your code, and you don't show up? Or I get your code and you don't meet us at this address?"

"That's a good question and I'm glad you asked. If ever I don't come home at night like I usually do. And I haven't called to tell you I'm not gonna be home. Get missing. And if I put the code in and then don't mee you at the address in New York immediately. Look for me at least for about two weeks. If I don't show, then you know what time it is.", he said looking her in the eyes.

Terrified now, she let him know so. 'I'm scared Telly."

"Have a drink.", he said handing her a full glass of Hennessy. "Don't worry boo. It's just a precaution. You feel me?"

Drinking down the glass of Hennessey. Once again for the second time that night. She didn't answer him.

Chapter 21

One of those rare nights out together off the job. The Broadie Boyz were rolling deep. Following each other in their luxury cars and trucks. Through the streets of South Philly towards one of the city's biggest arenas. In order to see Allen Inverson in action. Doing his signature flamboyant moves against the Los Angeles Lakers. Eager to witness the individual rivalry of the two teams superstars.

Driving himself in his money green Jaguar tonight. Broke was cruising in the midst of his army. Cars in the front and back of him. Situated for security sake so as to thwart any would be assassin. Animal in the passenger seat preoccupied with he car's CD Player. While Telly sat in the backseat as usual just watching the scenery as they passed through.

From the sounds of the loud music coming from their vehicles. All in different rhythms and sequences. Telly thought to himself that they sounded like an African ceremony. Where drummers pounded on bongos creating different beats. The mixtures of the bass being felt inside listeners bodies. Giving off the impression that at any moment. Something spectacular was getting ready to jump off.

On the few occasions they went out together like this. Telly always felt like he was in a pack of wolves. Out hunting in the wilderness under the fill moon. Apparently, he want the only one who felt that way. The look on pedestrians faces as they rode by. Told him they probably were thinking similar thoughts. Which was a testament to the vibe members gave of. Because the area they were in now. Wasn't even an area where they were known like that.

Feeling good from his usual syrup high. Licking his lips and looking with greedy eyes. Broke stared at the different crews on street corners. Posted up around flashy cars. Comfortable in their environments. "Yeah, I think its about time we introduced ourselves out here.", Broke said almost to himself. Hearing his voice, but not understanding Animal asked, "What?"

Glancing Animal's way he said, 'I think its about time we fixed our muscle out here. These South Philly niggas is getting money. I be peeping them out every time I'm out this way. Niggas seem like they carefree and shit. We gonna change that, watch."

Laughing Animal said playfully, "Broke you shell yo. Always eager to take something from somebody."

Piping in from the backseat Telly joked, "I know fam. Leave people alone sometimes."

When they laughed at his joke, it seemed to Telly it was strained laughter. Like the kind a person gives when they don't find something really funny. Although they laugh anyway just because. It was an understandable thing that happened to everybody. For some reason though, on this particular night it made Telly feel awkward.

As if sensing that Telly felt this way. Broke looked at Telly in the rearview mirror saying, "You a fool Telly. Always been a funny ass nigga. Even back in the day."

Smiling, Telly didn't respond. He just went back to looking out the window. Checking out a soldiers girlfriend in the car beside him. Busy taking deep pulls off a blunt. As her boyfriend controlled the Acura Legend with one hand. Nodding his head hard to the music pumping out his trunk.

In fifteen minutes they had made it to the Wachovia Arena parking lot. All members parking their vehicles as close as they could to the entrance. All hopping out with weapons in hand. Quickly tucking them out of sight. As they started to follow. Broke's lead towards the players entrance.

A puzzling look suddenly appeared on Telly's face. As he noticed all the uniformed police standing around. Tapping Animal on his arm he said, "Them police ain't gonna let us in with all these guns man. Ya'll ain't never been here before?"

Looking at him as if he was stupid. Then realizing Telly hadn't been down with them long enough to know. Animal just said, "Just chill, it's all good. You think we crazy?"

Stepping to a uniformed security guard outside the door. Broke greeted him with outstretched hand. "What's good Paul?"

Smiling the guard said, "Another day on the job Broke."

Then he immediately slid the yellow horse out the way. Allowing them to file in the entrance the ball players came in at. Causing Telly to tap himself on the forehead. As if to say of course. Regretting that stupid comment he made a few seconds ago.

He had been down with the team long enough to know. The power Broke wield throughout certain spots in the city. Money was power and her had firsthand knowledge on how much he had. Getting guns inside a basketball arena was nothing.

Navigating the corridors to the arenas waiting area. They made it to their box floor seats. Just as the announcer was introducing the players. Turning around to address his soldiers Broke said, "You know if some of ya'll want to, you can go up to the skybox and watch the game. I just like to be down here on the floor. Because I can see the game better. It make a nigga feel like Im at Duckery playground. Up in the skybox muthafucka's be looking like ants."

Several members changed directions. Taking their girlfriends hand and heading back the other way. More concerned to drink free champagne, then concerned about how well they could see the game. Telly and Animal really had no choice. Even when they were off the job, they were on the job. So they took seats each beside Broke settling in for what looked was going to be a good game.

Dribbling the autographed Sixers basketball that he got for his son. One of the Broadie Boyz did moves identical to Allen Iverson. As the crowds of people exited the Arena. Happy this night for the Sixers win by one point in O.T. Spinning into his girlfriend, the young man bumped her. Then stepped back as if he was taking a jump shot.

Reacting quickly before he could fully extend. His girl stripped the ball out his hands.

Everybody in the nearest vicinity laughed. Beside him Petey yelled, "You fake ass A.I.! Get yo ass to the muthafuckin car!"

Laughing along with everybody else. The young man snatched the ball from his girl and started towards the car. Walking backwards he asked aloud, "We going to Triple Five right?"

Hearing his question Animal said, "Yeah." Then looking at his watch Animal said, "Oh shit! My dogs fuck around and be hungry. If I don't shoot out there real quick. We'll meet you there. Ima head to the crib real fast." "Fuck it. I'll rock with you. I ain't in no rush. Plus I feel like driving anyway", Petey said.

Nodding his head Anima said, "That's all good. The rest of ya'll niggas though. Go ahead to Triple Five."

Climbing inside their vehicles. The bulk of the crew headed to the nightclub leaving only Broke's car and Petey and his passengers. Following each other to the Northeast section of Philly. An area that had a particularly wooden arena. Making it an ideal place for somebody like Animal who was a breeder of pitbulls.

Speeding down the expressway. Traffic was almost nonexistent once they got away from the arena. Leaning over behind Broke in the driver's seat. Telly stretched his leg to the other side of the car. Resting his head on the window frame. Closing his eyes in an attempt to relax a little.

Thirty minutes into their drive, Telly still hadn't moved much from his position. He wasn't sleep though. Because up in the front of the car. Telly clearly heard the sounds of them whispering. Although he couldn't make out what they were saying.

Whether because they weren't trying to disturb him out of respect or what. Telly really didn't know. What he did know though was. This whispering going on now. Was in several instances, tonight that seemed strange to him. The strained laughter earlier on in the night. The cool indifference from certain members he'd always been tight with. The way everytime he got up to go somewhere during the game. Somebody seemed to have somewhere to go too.

Like they were keeping an eye on him. Then all of a sudden out of the blue, something that never happened before as well as he knew. Animal needed to go home because he forgot to feed his dogs.

Far from a dummy. He knew just as well as he knew his name. It was going down tonight. They had figured out who was doing the stealing. Like je knew they eventually would. Just not this fast. Now they were getting ready to do god knows what. Probably torture him into telling where their money went. To say he was scared would be an understatement. Surrounded by the more vicious members of the crew, he was terrified.

Quickly his mind raced to find a way out. Feeling the vibrations from the car going down the expressway. He knew they were going too fast for him to jump out. Cracking his eyes alittleto look out the opposite window. He also noted he didn't know where he was at. Shutting them again in order to continue the façade of appearing sleep. Telly slid his hand under his shirt. Gripping the .9mm Taurus he had tucked in his waistband. Pulling it out where they couldn't see. He couldn't just raise up and start blasting. He knew the car was going too fast. What he was going to do was wait until the car stopped. Then using his knowledge as a surprise. He was going to jump out and blast Broke and Animal. Then run like hell hoping he could get away from the chase car. That held Petey and three other members. A part of his plan was to kill two top dogs anyway. That way, his chances of getting away would be easier. Once niggas started running around like chickens with their heads cut off.

Now he still had a chance to do it. Although the circumstances was slightly different. Heart pounding like a bass booster with now sweaty palms around his weapon. He cracked his eyes to keep an eye on what they were doing. While at the same time focusing on the motion of the car. Ready to hop out at the first opportunity.

In the front seat holding his weapon, a .44 Bulldog, animal heatedly whispered, "Let's just shrimp this nigga now. While he back there sleep. Nigga won't know what hit him."

Keeping his voice equally low with the same intensity, Broke said, "Hell naw, I want to make this nigga pay. Plus I want to know where my fucking money at. This nigga done stole damn near close to a million dollars."

"I done seen him in action fam. He strapped too. Trust me, you don't want to give him no daylight. Let's just be rid of him."

"Fuck that nigga. I want my money.", Broke whispered with a scowl. "Seven to one, that nigga can't stand it. I tell you what. As soon as I pull up in your driveway. Just be ready to put that hammer on him.

Before he even get out the car. He ain't that crazy to try some hero shit in the face of that barrel." Trying to hear what was being said. Still not able to fully understand though. Telly did catch one word "Driveway". He made it up in his mind then. He wouldn't wait that long. Whatever they meant by saying driveway. It couldn't be good. Feeling the rhythm of the car change underneath him. Telly watched as the Jaguar headed towards the exit. As far as he could see it wasn't nothing but woods. Common sense told him though. That's the house where they were headed was probably nearby. So he decided to make his move. Just as soon as Broke stopped at the intersection. Like everybody did when taking an exit off the freeway.

Reaching behind him Telly flicked the door switch quietly. Then patiently waited with his hand on the door handle. When the Jaguar started to slow. He flicked the safety on his weapon. Then as if came to stop. He pulled the handle and fell out the car backwards. Squeezing off a shot directly at Animal's head.

As he slid across the asphalt on his back. Animal's brains flew all over the front windshield. Causing Broke to immediately pull his weapon. Aiming out the windshield of the driver's side door with his foot on the brake. Towards Telly jumping to his feet quickly. Trading a few shots using the cover of the car for advantage. Still taking two shots in his chest area though. Sending the car drifting into the intersection slowly, out of control.

Cringing from the shot he took in his right leg. Telly turned and sprinted towards the woods. Halfway there he heard the familiar spray of a Mac II. Literally he could hear shells whistle past as he picked up speed. Hoping he could lose the five other men in the darkness.

Out of breath from the pressure of the slugs, but okay because he was vested up. Broke slammed his foot down on the brakes before he came to any type of accident. Pushed the gear shift into park. Then looking at Animal who was a mess slumped dead on the passenger seat with gun still in hand. With uncontrollable fury in his eyes. He jumped out the car and joined his members on the case.

Telly could feel the blood pouring out his wounds. Sliding down his leg into his Timberland boots, ruining them. His whole right leg was already beginning to get cold. He knew it was just a flesh wound though. Simply because in spite of the injury. He was still able to more his leg. Stumbling through wooded area now. He was grateful for the cover it provided. As the men following him around aimed shots at him. Knowing just as well as he did. Their chances were slim trying to catch him in that darkness.

Tripping over branched and shambles every few feet. Telly still kept running towards the woods interior. Even once letting off a shot to slow his pursuers progress. From the sound of snapping twigs in the distance. He could tell they were having as hard a time as him. He hoped that would be a discouraging factor. As he pushed deeper and deeper inside. The sounds from the pursuers suddenly stopped. Standing still now be listened to the sounds of the night. The screeching of tires told him they had given up chase. However, he was under no illusion that they had given up on him. Falling to the ground he took a look at his leg.

Getting his pants down so he could get a look at it. Remembering somethings about pressure points he read in Tanya's nurse books. He applied pressure on the femoral artery in the groin. It took several tries, but slowly the blood flow started to slow. Taking his shirt off in order to get to the wife beater underneath. He firmly tied the t-shirt in a knot in front of the wound.

After being sure it was tight enough. He got himself together then begun his trek again. Knowing from experience of the Northeast section of Philly. That wooded area could only be so much deep. Before giving way to some homes out this area. He found his knowledge correct after about ten more minutes. Coming out onto a residential street lined with big two story homes.

Just as he emerged into the clearing. His luck couldn't have been any better. Coming down the street he saw a black woman in her car. Running out in front of the car with a limp. He flagged down the woman. When she hoped out to come to his aid. He pulled his gun forcing her down on the asphalt. Then jumped inside her running car and drove off. Pushing the small Toyota as fast as it could go.

Having used up all his luck for tonight. It took him over a half hour before he came to a gas station. Almost hysterical with worry now. He climbed out and ran to the nearest phone. Fished inside his pocket for the right change. Then dialed Tanya's pager and put in the code.

Chapter 22

In a sixty-nine position Tanya sucked on Greg's dick with gusto. Taking his full length deep inside her throat. Tightening her lips as much as possible around his shaft. As she felt his tongue slide deeper inside of her. Caressing her pussy as only he could. Sending shivers of pleasure throughout her whole body. Motivating her to try and return the favor.

Sliding her lips up to the head of his dick. Tanya leaned forward just enough. In order to envelope his dick between her perky breasts. Then started to rub it vigorously up and down. While simultaneously twisting her lips around his head. Eager to taste his cum in her mouth. As she felt herself rising to a powerful climax.

Pressing her pussy hard against his mouth. Even with her mouth full, her moan sounded loud. As she came on his stroking tongue. Then as if by willpower alone. While she was still in the throes of pleasure. Greg exploded inside her warm mouth. As she ran the back of her tongue across his opening. Licking up every drop as fast as it came. Rubbing his shaft up and down with her soft breasts. Forcing him to empty it all.

When she was completely satisfied. Without hesitation she mounted him in reverse cowgirl style. Bouncing her pretty ass up and down on top. Gripping her breasts with both hands. As from behind he palmed both her ass cheeks. Spreading them open just enough. To enable him to watch as his shaft penetrated in and out her. Disappearing completely when she slammed herself down. Eyes closed in her passion. Adjusting her rhythm to his now upwards thrusts. At first she chose to ignore the sound of her pager. As if it echoed out loud sitting on top of her discarded clothes. Then as if by intuition or just plain common sense. Being as though few people had her pager number. She opened her eyes reluctantly and slid off him. To his utmost disappointment. Walking naked over to her pager to see hear was going on.

Bending over without bending her knees, she grabbed the pager. Hitting the button and looking at the little screen. The number 999 showed on the screen. Starring at it for a few seconds her eyes got wider. Her nightmare ever since Telly had gave her this code several days ago. Suddenly had come true. Just like that gone was the mood she had moments ago. In its place was the terrified feeling she felt that night.

Without even turning around she quickly started dressing. Letting out a frustrated sigh Greg asked, "What's going on?"

Facing him but still getting dressed she answered, "You go to go. I'm sorry. It's an emergency."

Leaning up in the guestroom bed. The first thing that came to his mind. Was that her boyfriend was on his way home. He had been over Tanya's house secretly several times now. Never finding himself in a position where he had to rush out. Due to Tanya's careful planning. Making sure her daughter wasn't present, etc.

Smiling he found himself welcoming a confrontation now. Ever since his phone call to the local F.B.I. Putting them onto Telly's sudden extravagance. He knew Telly's days were numbered. Might as well let the nigga see who was fucking his girl. Greg thought to himself feeling cocky. More logically thinking though he knew better to attempt that.

Before he could confirm his assumption. Tanya was dressed and quickly walking out the room. Down the hallway towards the master bedroom. Shutting and locking the door behind her. So Greg couldn't see what she was doing. Then she grabbed a blue gym bag out the closet and headed to the safe in the bathroom. Opening it wide and stacking money in the bag. Planning in her head the next move to make. Concerning picking up Tahira from her mothers house. Then getting out of the city as fast as she could.

She really didn't know what to expect. All she could really go off of. Was the seriousness in the way things was explained to her. So she was going to just follow his directions to the letter....

Feeling guilty again about her infidelity. As once again reality was placed squarely in her face. On how much Telly loved her. As well as how much he was sacrificing to make sure they were good. Out there risking his life. She was kind of happy they would be moving on. Hopefully it would be truly a new beginning for them as a family.

They had to take Animal's body out the car. Then, leave it out front of a hospital. Simply because it would be too many questions to answer. If he did it any other way. What a way to have to do a childhood friend Broke thought. Slamming his fist down on the Jaguar's steering wheel for the umpteenth time. His fury was still uncontrollable. Concerning the events that had taken place tonight.

Words couldn't describe the things he wanted to do to Telly. Death was too easy for a muthafucka like that. What in the world possessed him to do what he did? Didn't he show that nigga nothing but love? The money he was paying Telly on a regular basis. Was money that some people didn't see in a lifetime. Even some that had degrees from college didn't make that much money as fast. So he just couldn't understand it. Now his right hand man was dead. He now truly felt like the last man standing.

Animal was one hundred percent right. When he suggested they should just go ahead and kill Telly. He regretted not taking up that suggestion now. Looking at his reflection in the rearview mirror. Seeing the expression on his face. Broke suddenly checked the avenue his thoughts were taking. He seemed to be slipping from anger to guilt. At this recognition suddenly his anger returned. Telly had made him look like a fool three times.

One, for embracing a shiesty ass nigga like that. Breaking bread and putting him on his feet. Two, for stealing money right out from under his nose. After being placed in a position of trust. And three, for escaping him in this night. Also, in the process killing a life long friend.

Gripping the steering wheel tightly. This open display of anger was uncharacteristic of him. He was usually the one who had the upper hand. The one in supreme control. Making the next person mad. Out maneuver his adversary. Not the other way around. The way it was with Telly at this particular moment.

Forcing himself to calm down. He glanced at the clock on his dashboard. The time read fifteen until twelve midnight. Over about forty minutes ago. When they all jumped back in their cars and sped away. He had called his soldiers on the car phone. Sending the men out to Telly's home to kidnap his family. He may not know where Telly was at. But he had an idea on how to find him. His family was the key. He wondered how they were doing...

Looking at the piece of paper with Telly's address on it. Something they bring along in order to help persuade information out of Telly. Once they began the torture session planned. Broke allowed himself a small smirk. Thinking he may yet have the upper hand.

Reaching over to the partially cleaned glove compartment. Where he had scrubbed away the dried blood as best he could. He pulled it open and extracted a bottle of yellow syrup. Closing the compartment back shut. He drank down the syrup as he headed towards his condo.

Hearing the knob to the bedroom door turn. Tanya hurried to stack the last of the money in the bag. "I'll be right there", she called out.

Zipping the bag shut. She then closed the safe and fixed everything back the way it was. Then carried the bag into the bedroom. Placing it out of sight near the far side of the bed. Opening the door she said, "I told you, I have to go."

"Damn its an emergency like that. You got to lock the doors and everything. I'm just saying goodbye", he said wrapping his arms around her waist. French kissing him with the passion of a person saying their last goodbye. Tanya let her hands wander underneath his balls. Before pulling back saying with finality, "Alright we done wasted enough time."

Noticing she didn't say when they would see each other again. Which was something she normally did after their meetings. For a few seconds Greg just stared at her. Studying the expression on her face. Feeling with the instinct of a long time acquaintance. The truth of the situation without her having to tell him.

Still his emotions for her wouldn't accept it. He had to hear it from her mouth. "So when Ima see you again?", he asked.

Not trying to waste anymore time. Figuring correctly that telling the truth would only make their departure longer. She turned on her charm. "Probably on Wednesday after work. Why you looking like that? It's just a family emergency, and I really have to go. Your holding me up. Go on and let yourself out while I grab some things."

Confused a little now. Wondering if his instincts were wrong. He decided to just let it go. Thinking he might have judged wrong. The expression on her face was probably because of the emergency she was talking about.

"Aiight then shorty. I'm gone."

Walking down the hallway he headed down the staircase. Entering the front room he stopped to admire the paintings on the wall. Getting that feeling of jealousy again. That he always felt when comparing his financial status with Telly's. Then after a few minutes, he headed across the spacious room towards the front door.

Lifting the gym bag up. Placing the strap across her body to ease the weight. Tanya took one last glance at the first home she ever owned. Eyes roaming across the bedroom with memories. Then without hesitation she turned out the lights and hurried towards the staircase.

Before Greg could reach the front door. Suddenly the door came swinging in on it's hinges. Crashing up against the wall. While simultaneously two masked men holding guns came rushing inside. The one with the Mossberg pump let the shot gun boom. Instantly parts of Greg's head flew in different directions. Fragments of his skull hit the ground even before his body did. Knowing they were only here to grab the daughter and mother. The man with the pump kicked the headless body to the floor saying, "Get the fuck out the way."

Seasoned spot rushers as these men were. Without even breaking their stride. Both men started to scan the room. One with a SKS assault rifle and the other with a .12 gauge shotgun. Each side by side looking in different directions. Alert for the slightest movement. Eager to do their job and leave. Knowing this wasn't the kind of neighborhood used to hearing gunshots in the middle of the night.

Her heart almost stopped beating from fear. Upon hearing the loud sounds of the shotgun echo off the walls. Frozen with fear at the moment. She didn't know what to do. Then out of panic, more than out of making a decision. She ran back upstairs stopping in the hallway. Looking up at the entrance to the attic. Debating whether to hide up there or not. Every few seconds glancing back towards the stairs.

Dismissing that spot for a place to hide. Thinking it would be too obvious once the men made it upstairs. She ran into their bedroom. Sliding one of the windows up that was situated in the room. Sticking her head out to check the distance to the ground. Immediately recognizing the dangers of attempting a jump like that.

Pulling herself back in, she turned and faced the bed. Looking at the sheet on top of it. She wondered if she could make a rope out of them. Wondered if she had enough time.... Sounds coming from downstairs told her she didn't. As she listened, she could hear the sound of the men. Coming slowly up the stairs. Looking back towards the open window. She resigned herself to jump. Better than let these men get a hold of her.

Turning back in its direction. She grabbed the ledge on the windowsill. Then suddenly a better idea popped in her mind. Reaching towards the drawer of the nightstand by the bed. She pulled it open and grabbed the .45 handgun. Telly kept inside. Closing the drawer back, she ran to their closet, slid the mirrored door closed behind her, and navigated her way back to a section that was added on by the previous owners. A crawl space used to keep boxes of shoes so as to limit the space inside.

Quickly she pulled box after box out. Stacking them along the wall neatly. So, she wouldn't give herself away. Then after stuffing the bag of money inside. She wiggled herself in backwards. Pulling as many shoe boxes as she could. Up against the open spot to cover the entrance. Until the crawl space located in the back of the closet. Could hardly be noticed. Or so she desperately hoped.

From her spot inside the crawl space. She could hear the men upstairs rushing from room to room now. Slamming door and flipping over beds. Their search becoming much more earnest. As the sounds of police sirens wafted throughout the night air. Warning whoever it concerned of its soon arrival.

Mouthing a silent prayer she hadn't said since she was young. Tanya almost willed the police to make it soon. Clutching the .45 in her left hand. Tanya scrunched herself up as small as she could. Steady listening as the sound pf the searching men got closer.

In the bedroom now, one of the men checked in the bathroom. Coming back out after checking he said in frustration, "These muthafucka's ain't even here." Opening the closet door and scanning it with his eyes. The man with the shotgun said, "Then who is that muthafucka downstairs. Something don't seem right."

Hearing the sirens through the open window getting closer. The other man said, "Yeah I know. Is this the right address?"

Stepping inside the closet sliding some clothes out the way. The man with the pump answered, "Yeah I double checked. This the right house." Then pausing for a second he stared at the stacked shoeboxes in the back. "Broke told me the address over the phone three times. He sounded like he wanted Telly bad yo. So I doubt he made a mistake."

The sounds from the police starting to unnerve him. The man with the rifle stated, "Fuck it. They ain't here. Let's get the fuck out of here. The police sound like they getting real close."

"Hold up", the one with the pump said. Walking over to where the shoe boxes were stacked.

Looking around his partner at the empty closet. With an irritated voice the rifle man said, "Man fuck that shit. I'm gone."

Starring at the shoeboxes for one more second. His partners anxiousness to leave became contagious. Backing out the closet. He ran through the house to catch up with him. In about three minutes an engine could be heard starting up outside.

As if she had been holding her breath all that time. Tanya let outa long sigh. Still so much scared up. That she stayed right in that crawl space until shortly afterwards the police arrived.

Chapter 23

Staring at a big black cockroach crawling across the wall. Only able to be seen from the streetlights illumination outside the apartment window. Telly sat in the dark inhaling blunt smoke. Trying to ease the pain that was throbbing through his leg. Because he didn't plan on going to the hospital. Until he was with his family out in New York City. He hoped his leg would stand up.

Still hysterical with worry. He prayed his small family was okay. He really had no way of knowing right now. Everything would be made clear tomorrow. Right now he was laying low in their old apartment down Susquehanna. When they moved into their new house. He never stopped paying rent. Figuring he might need a place to crash one night. When he didn't feel like driving all the way out to the suburbs.

Later on considerably down the line. He found the apartment played a convenient role in his plans. With the safe at his home being about full. He had started to stash the rest of the money in here. Plus he could get to it fast. Whenever he made his rounds. Laying across the bed now, was five hundred thousand dollars in stolen money.

Putting the remaining blunt out of his shoe. Telly walked over to the bed and began to bag the money up. Placing it in an old bookbag of his daughters to be ready to go, once he woke up. Leaving the city of Brotherly Love behind forever. Starting a new life in the "City of Dreams"

Once everything was packed inside. He layed the bag on the other side of the bed. Placed his gun within arms reach. Then in a fit of exhaustion. Layed down fully clothed to get some needed rest. The roaches crawling across the sheets and pillows. Didn't hardly bother him. In a few minutes, he was sound asleep. No doubt dreaming of a brighter future.

The rest of the night was uneventful. And around dawn, Telly was still fitfully asleep. When suddenly the sound of the flimsy door being kicked in awoke him out his sleep. Through his groggy brain he heard sounds of heavy feet stomping across the small apartment. No question in search of him.

In a state of shock and defeat. Telly turned to grab his .9mm Taurus that lay beside him on the bed. The same gun that served him so well the night before. Although before he could turn back around. The heavy feet were inside his room. Crowding around the bed so they could see him with guns drawn. Terror had complete control over his body. As he looked at their masked faces in the semi-dark room. The idea of dying looming heavy in his mind. Then the man closest to him holding a submachine gun screamed, "DON'T MOVE!!!! F.B.I.!!"

Smiling, right then at that moment. Those words were the sweetest he ever heard.

Pain in his chest where the bullets struck ten times worse now. Sitting up in bed, Broke gasped for breath. Wondering if maybe he had a slight fracture in his rib cage. From the pressure of the slugs that impacted his vest last night. Glancing out his bedroom window. From the shadow blue texture of sky he could tell it was around dawn. Feeling like he had just laid down to rest about an hour ago. Even though he had about six hours of rest. Broke wished he could put off the responsibilities of the day. He had so much on his agenda. Just thinking about them made him feel overwhelmed.

Climbing over to the edge of his bed. He reached for the telephone on his nightstand. His mind already cleaning out the mental cobwebs. Despite his physical reluctance to start the day. As he placed the receiver against his ear. Tapping the rectangular button to bring up a dial tone.

After about five or six taps and still not hearing a dial tone. Broke looked at the phone with curiosity. Wondering if it was broken or something. Then his eyes glanced to the digital clock beside it.

Noticing the small screen was blank of its usual red digits. Tapping the buttons on it trying to get a response. The moment of curiosity suddenly turned into irritation.

Clad in boxer shorts and bare chested. He stepped into his combat boots positioned by the bed. Then walked downstairs into another room in search of a phone to use. Finding one, he reached for it finding the same thing as in his bedroom. Looking around that room to check the electrical appliances as well. He saw that a lamp he knew he left on last night was turned off. Vague realization of the situation kicked in.

Out loud he said to himself in disappointment, "Ain't this a bitch. When it rains it pours. The fucking powers out at a time when I badly need the phone. Just my luck."

Heading back towards his bedroom, in midmotion he stopped. Standing perfectly still he listened for an odd sound he had just heard. In a matter of seconds, he heard it again. Thumping sounds coming from the hallway outside his front door. Sounding as if a crowd of people were all walking at once. Making irregular movements as if moving in stealth.

He didn't know what was going on. Nor did he waste any time trying to figure it out. Irregular movements outside his hallway at the same time the power being out, was enough to get him on point. Immediately he ran back upstairs towards his bedroom. Eager to get the weaponry he kept inside. Stashed in his walk in closet.

By the time he made it in his bedroom. And was slamming the thirty round reddish plastic magazine up into his AK-47. The sounds of the battering ram banging against his door echoed throughout the spacious condo. After two more determined swings. The thick expensive door came crashing in. Falling straight down to the ground. As if it was nothing but paper.

Moving in fast the point man yelled, "A.T.F!!! A.T.F.!!!"

From his cover at the top of the stairwell now. Broke answered his exclamation with a spray of the AK on fully auto. Raking slugs across the room from left to right. As more federal Agents came pouring in. A few falling right where they stood. While the rest assessed the situation and returned fire. Equally matched to this confrontation with the automatic weapons as well.

Chunks from the plastered wall dislodged and sprayed in Broke's face. Upon feeling the impact of the AR-15s unleashed power. Pulling back out the way. He released the magazine and slammed another home. Switching his weapon to semi-auto. Without glancing he stuck his arm around the corner, letting off a few shots intent on keeping them back.

Seeing he had the better position being on higher ground. The agents pulled back out the condo. Dragging their wounded partners with them. Not eager to force the situation. Knowing about his access to weaponry. Figuring logically that it wasn't no telling what he had up there. It was a possibility he could have a bazooka up there.

Waiting for return fire that never came. After about five minutes Broke took a quick peek. Darting his head around the corner, then back again. Adrenaline pumping like crazy. He knew they were still out there and wasn't going away. They weren't some street hooligans attempting an assassination. There were Federal Agents hellbent on his arrest. He heard the man loud and clear when he screamed his identification.

In frustration he said, "Goddamn it."

He knew he was trapped. There wasn't no way out but by the front door. His condo was located sixteen floors above the ground. What was he going to do?.....

Surrender and place his trust in the high priced lawyers he retained?....

A few moments thought almost bring him to laughter. Here he was shooting it out with Federal Agents. Who most likely had an airtight case against him. And he was thinking about putting faith in lawyers.

How preposterous! He knew in his gut right there and then. Wasn't no amount of money going to be able to get him out this shit.

Staring at his weapon. It didn't take long to make his choice. It didn't take the Federal Agents long either to regroup. In his moment of indecision. A special team of agents had already reentered the room. Geared up in gas masks equipped with flash grenades. That they sent sailing up the steps before them. Exploding on impact temporarily blinding Broke. As they followed up with tear gas canisters. Running top speed along side it.

The combination was too much for Broke to handle. Stumbling back away from the stairs blindly. Coughing from the tear gas. Through his hearing he listened for their approach, then emptied out the rest of his magazine. When he thought they were at the top. His slugs found one agent who fell over to his side. The ones behind him returned fire. Raking Broke's right side with the shells. Causing him to drop to the ground as well.

As if by teleportation, instantly, they were standing over top of him. One kicking the AK out his clutched hand. One aiming his assault rifle down on him. While another bent down, turning him over on his stomach. Securing him with plastic handcuffs. Not really wanting to being as through Broke had just tried to kill them. But knowing it was all apart of the job. Seeing the Broke was still breathing. The Agent screamed in his radio for a medic to arrive. One for his partner, and the other for the suspect.

Running like a bat out of hell. As soon as he saw the first S.W.A.T. Team truck turn the corner. The lookout for the stash house out in West Philly came busting in the door bringing all conversation to a stop. Out of breath he informed, "The police out there. A S.W.A.T. team and everything."

With raised eyebrows Petey said, "A S.W.A.T. Team."

"Word", the lookout responded.

Hands cupped around his mouth Petey screamed upstairs, "Five-O! Five-O! Everybody ger the fuck out of here!"

It was too late for that though. Several city blocks in the vicinity were already cordoned off. In anticipation of ant attempted flight. That's why they didn't try and catch the lookout off guard. In fact, they wanted to be seen. In hopes of discouraging a gun battle through the show of force. That's why this dawn raid was a snake attack like the others that had taken place of Telly and Broke.

This tactic of a show of force was being used simultaneously at all the Broadie Boyz stash houses across the city. It was a joint venture being undertaken by Federal and local officials.

As the feds finally ended their thirty-six month investigation. Rounding up as many members as they could find.

Stepping to the window to lookout. Before they all rushed out the door. Thoughts of running out swiftly left Petey's mind. When he saw all the members of law enforcement up and down the block. They had people with A.T.F. identification on. People with F.B.I. identification on. Plus across the street on top of the roof. A man laid on his stomach with a S.W.A.T. team suit on. Aiming a rifle with a scope at the house they were in.

Seeing that Petey moved back away from the window. Pointing to the man at the end of the crowd he ordered, "Look out that window and tell me what you see out back."

The man's exclamation of Goddamn!" when he checked. Was all the info Petey needed to hear upon making his decision. "Aiight ya'll. Its going down. The police is outside cray deep for us. I'm banging out, but ya'll don't have to. Anybody that want to surrender go ahead and do so now."

Looking at each other. They waited for somebody to step up. After a long wait two members stepped out the crowd, and headed towards the door. Where Petey stood waiting for them. Punching one in the jaw and hitting the other across the temple. Laying them both flat on the floor. "Yeah, now we got hostages. I was just weeding out the weak. The rest of ya'll start barricading the windows and doors. And take up position where your able to shoot back." Motioning with his hands to the lookout. "You tie these clowns up and afterwards bring up all the guns."

Setting about doing what they were told to do. Stacking every available piece of furniture up against windows and doors. When they were about halfway through, a megaphone sounded outside, "All occupants inside 9271 come out with your hands up! I repeat all occupants in 9271 come out with your hands up now!"

Stepping to the window making sure he stayed out if sight. Petey yelled back, "We got hostages and we ain't coming out!"

Amused at his comment because they knew everybody that was in the house. Knowing them to all be members of the Broadie Boyz. They didn't even respond. Plus even if they did have legitimate hostages. They had no intentional of going in anytime soon.

Aware of the firepower the occupants held. Their first choice was to force a surrender. Then if need be, it would be a reenactment of MOVE in the 21st century. When authorities literally bombed a house holding back revolutionaries. Causing blocks of houses to burn down in the process.

Taking the authorities, no response as disrespect. Petey grabbed a Mac-90 leaning up against the wall. Then with no further ado, sprayed shots out the window. Setting off the inevitable confrontation that was building up.

Chapter 24

Laying in the bed in the infirmary of the Federal Detention Center in Philadelphia. Telly peeked under the sheets at his still hurting leg. Making sure the bandages weren't bunched up from rough sleep. Seeing it was okay, he laid back again. Closing his eyes in an attempt to catch a few more minutes of rest. Before getting up to start his day.

Rubbing his sore leg absently. He thought to himself. It was a good thing that he got the medical attention he needed at the time. The doctors that did surgery on him four days ago, told him that the wound was so badly infected, just a couple of hours longer, and he would have lost his leg.

Would it have really mattered? Everything else was lost to him. The money he had when the feds rushed his spots. The house and car he brought. The accounts he set up for his daughter with the stolen money. As well as what looked to be his freedom for the rest of his life.

The only money he possibly had right now, was the money that Tanya had out in New York. If that was where she was at. He hadn't heard nothing from her since he got locked up. He didn't know if she was alive or dead. In good health or sick. He had only been in custody for five days now. Still though she should have still got in touch.

Then again, maybe she didn't know. He didn't know how the newspapers were out in New York. What was mega news in Philly probably wasn't so big a deal in New York. He doubted it though. Because in all his years on Earth, he had never seen such media coverage devoted to an organization. The members of the Broadie Boyz were all over the television and newspaper. They made them out to be bigger than the Mafia.

Opening his eyes he reached down to his cell floor, grabbing the article he cut out the newspaper. Detailing and arrests of their members. Reading them over again. He came to the conclusion that maybe they were bigger than the Mafia in a sense. Not because of the fifty-three murders, thirty attempted murders, and numerous extortion and robbery charges they were alleged to be responsible for. Nor the gun connect Broke had down south, who happened to be a former Green Beret. Nor the millions of dollars they were making on a regular basis. But more because of the way they went out.

Almost every arrest that was made ended in a full blown shootout. Resulting in numerous members deaths. Petey, Killa, and others. As well as some from law enforcement. Mafia members didn't go out like that. They surrender and tried to beat cases in court. The Broadie Boyz banged all the way out. Whether because of their access to firepower or what. Telly felt they were bigger than the Mafia in that sense.

Putting the article back down. Telly got up and limped his way to his commode. Which had a sink placed on top. Then began his hygiene. Looking at his reflection in the warped mirror above. Seeing no trace of the smile he wore when the Feds got him. Happy it was them and not the Broadie Boyz. Now he found himself wondering if that wouldn't have been a better fate. He knew he was never going home.

In the midst of brushing his teeth. He heard a knock at this cell door. Turing around with a toothbrush in mouth. He saw a white male guard standing outside saying, "Mr. Williams, you got a visit lets go."

Not feeling the tone of the guards voice he responded gruffly, "Aiight yo. Let me finished brushing my teeth first."

"Aiight you got about five minutes. If you not ready by then. Ima take it as a refusal.", the guard said before walking away.

"You fucking cracker", Telly said out loud.

If the guard heard, he didn't respond. In the meantime Telly hurry up. Being as though he didn't know who was visiting. And if he fuck around and missed a visit from Tanya. He was definitely going to spazz the fuck out.

By the time he was placing on his state boots. The guard was back opening his trap door saying, "Alright Williams its time. Turn around and place your hands out the trap." Once the handcuffs were placed on, the guard yelled, "Open F2-28."

As the sliding door slid open. Telly limped out handcuffed and joined the line of other prisoners going to visits. Walking through the hallways down to the bottom floor. Where they had non-contact visitation booths. Getting their handcuffs taken off once they entered.

Sitting down on a metal stool as the guard locked him inside. Telly stared through the plexiglass window with small holes in it. Watching other prisoners visitors walk by. Peeping in doors, trying to find their people. Until after about ten minutes of waiting. The door across the plexiglass window opened slowly. Revealing not Tanya who he had expected. But two muscular built black men. Both dressed in dark colored suits. Walking inside to seat themselves on the opposite stools.

The one placing a thick briefcase in front of him was the first to speak.

"How you doing Telly? How's the leg? My name is Special Agent Thomas and I'm with Alcohol, Tobacco, and Firearms Bureau." Waving his hand to the left. "This here is Special Agent Baker and he's with Federal Bureau of Investigation. We are here today to give you an opportunity to help yourself."

Leaning up on his elbow Telly asked, "What you mean "help myself"?

Then added, "Ya'll not even supposed to be talking to me without my lawyer present."

Not immediately answering his question. Agent Thomas reached inside the thick briefcase pulling out two yellowish colored folders. Placing them side by side before answering, "I mean exactly that. Helping yourself." Then, pointing to the largest folder he said, "You see this here? This is all the reports of the illegal activities of the Broadie Boyz. Thirty-six months of investigation." Then pointing to the other folder alittle less thick he said, :This is a report on all your illegal activities. Since coming home from prison and joining the Broadie

Boyz. Including the killing of Frankie Washington. You probably didn't know his name. But that's the guy you killed to become a member. Remember him?"

Anger being clearly heard in his voice Telly said, "So what the fuck you telling me this shit for. And what does it have to do with helping myself?"

"I'm telling you this Telly. Because you and every last other member of that organization is fucked. Unless you give us some kind of cooperation. I promised you will be buried alive with the rest of them."

"You got all those files sitting in front of you. What you need me for?"

"We need you to help corroborate some things I know only top member know. We are trying to seek the death penalty with Broke. And we are trying to help you help yourself. In the form of getting a sentence reduction for your cooperation. Because face it Telly, you gonna get some time. But you don't have to be behind bard forever. All you have to do is help us with a few things. And you got my word....We'll make a recommendation to the judge to get you back in court, and a reduced sentence guaranteed."

"I don't know what you muthafucka's is smoking! But ya'll got me fucked up! I ain't no snitch! Never have and never will!", Telly said in a loud voice.

Speaking for the first time with an equally loud voice, Agent Baker said, "Don't be stupid man! Them pieces of shit don't give a fuck about you! Or nobody else! You saw what they do to their own! What they tried to do to you! They even went after your family! And I guarantee once Broke is well, which the doctors say he is expected to make a full recovery, they'll be coming at you again!"

Calming down a little he said, "You'll be watching your back for the rest of you life in prison. Don't be dumb. Think about your family Telly. These psychopaths don't deserve your loyalty."

"Hold up yo. Hold up. What you mean they went after my family?"

Feeling like they had him now. If they could effectively use this attempt on his family correctly. Before Baker could answer, Agent Thomas spoke out. "You don't know? Oh of course you don't know. That's the same night they tried to kill you...Well you already know how they are. So it should be no surprise they tried to kidnap your girl and daughter. Killing a man named Greg Hayes in the process."

"And this is the kind of muthafucka you trying to protect?", Agent Baker added.

"Are they okay? Did my girl and daughter get hurt?"

"From what I hear, their fine. A local policeman drove to her mothers house after the report."

"She might not be so lucky next time.", interjecting matter of factly.

Standing up from where he was seated. In his orange jumpsuit and state boots. Telly started to pace the small area. Looking as if the Federal Agents weren't even in the room. Thinking about the whole situation from beginning to end. How he really didn't know what he was getting into. Until it was too late. So eager to make a fortune that he didn't realize the stakes. Didn't understand the price he would have to pay to get it.

Stopping in midstride he remained standing. "Can I get back with ya'll. I got to think on it."

Seeing progress be made quickly Agent Thomas said, "Sure sure. No problem. We'll come back tomorrow to see you again."

"Aiight then. See you tomorrow", he said dismissively.

Immediately he got back to pacing the box. Back and forth as the agents left of the room. Leaving him alone, feeling like a lion at the zoo. Pacing around his shit infested cage.

Driving a Toyota Camry rental car that she got from a rental place in lower Manhattan. Tanya cruised down the turnpike headed towards Philly. In order to visit Telly for the first time to find out what she needed to do to help. Either to get a lawyer, bail money, or get into some gangsta shit. It really didn't matter to her. All she wanted was him home with her.

In the passenger seat beside her, Tahira sat quietly looking out the window. At the age she was now, she was old enough to understand the seriousness of the situation. No matter how much her mother tried to ease her concerns from the things she read in the newspaper and saw on T.V., she knew the chances of her dad getting out of this was slim. And deep inside she was hurting bad. Having bonded with her father when he came back home.

Glancing her daughter's way while driving. Through mothers intuition, she felt her pain. She just didn't know what to say. How could you tell a little girl at the age of ten that it's a one percent chance your father is ever coming home again. That the only relationship you will have with him for the remainder of your life would be prison visitation days. For a couple of hours per week maybe. If the administration didn't decide to send him somewhere far away.

So instead, she told her that ne would be able to get out of this. That he couldn't possibly be responsible for all those murders. Having come home just that year. She even had showed her all the money they had. Giving her assurance that Telly would have the best lawyers money could buy. She told her everything, but the truth.

To be absolutely honest. She wasn't quite ready to face the truth either. Here she was yet again. Alone out in the world by herself. Yeah financially things were completely different. Still though, the man she loved and wanted to be with was out of reach again.

Coming into Philadelphia's city limit now, seeing Americas fifth largest city skyline. She started to think about the events that took place. Where Greg got killed in her home. Leaving this world in such a violent way. That she thought he didn't deserve. Wondering how much Telly knew about that. Suddenly feeling a little apprehension concerning their visit. Hoping that if he did know about it, the importance of the other things would take first priority. Leaving that occurrence to simply fade into the background.

Recognizing the landmarks as they drove by them, Tahira asked, "When we coming home?"

"I don't know sweetheart. I have to talk to your father and see what he says."

She was wondering about that herself. Now that it seemed that whoever he crossed was locked up. Was it safe for them to come back in the city? Were their lives still in danger? She prayed it wasn't. The complete terror she felt when the men came looking for her was definitely something she didn't want to experience again. She hated to think of what she would have done. If Tahira was home with her that night and they were forced to hide.

Stopping at a stoplight. She checked for traffic before making a right turn. Then headed down a one way street. Towards a building that housed Federal prisoners. Situated on the farthest end of an enormous parking lot. Which she pulled into and found a spot.

Coming out the rental car. She held Tahira's hand as they walked across the parking lot. Mingling with the other visitors come to see their people as well. When the stepped inside, Tanya immediately placed their valuables in a foot locker without being told. Knowing the drill from years of visiting Telly in state prisons.

Waiting in line for several minutes. When it was their turn to approach the control booth, Tanya said, "I'm here to see Telly Williams."

Visibly tensing up as if she had been smacked. A black woman guard asked, "May I see some identification?"

Noticing how tense the woman had just got. Tanya handed her drivers license through a small slot. Watching as the guard looked it over, then got a phone and called somebody. Staying in conversation with whoever was on the line. Much longer it seemed to Tanya to let whoever was needed to know that Telly had a visitor.

Still holding the phone in her hand. The guard handed her back her identification asking politely, "May I ask what's your relation to Mr. Williams?"

"Im the mother of his child", she said looking at Tahira.

Nodding her head in comprehension. The guard said something into the phone before hanging up. "Okay Miss Talbert. Can you please wait over there. And shortly someone will be here to escort you."

Standing where she was told to stand. Still holding Tahira's hand. Tanya looked at the grayish walls. Slight depression slowly starting to creep in her thoughts. She always felt like this whenever she came to see him. Not only because of the fact he was incarcerated, also because of the make-up of the prisoners. Always finding wherever she went Black men and their families in the majority.

Cutting her off from her thoughts, a tall white man in uniform asked, "Are you Miss. Talbert?"

"Yes I am.", she answered with a nod.

"If you would please follow me. I'll take you to your visit."

Following the guard without saying a word. As they navigated through the corridors Tanya glanced at Tahira. Wondering if it was a good idea to bring her. What if things were said counterproductive to what she told her? Or God forbid the subject of Greg?

Stepping in front of a steel door with a glass window in it. The guard pulled out some keys and unlocked it. Opening the door, he smiled saying, "Have a nice visit. Just press that button whenever you're ready to leave."

Seeing his daughter step inside the box that was separated by a think plexiglass. Some of the tension he felt resolved. He thought it was some more cops come to visit. And was ready to spazz if they approached him on some more snitch shit.

After being taken back to his cell when he was done talking to the agents. It was only an hour later before they called him again. Informing his he had another visitor. In between that time, he was just sitting the. Thinking on how he could play the agents. Then at the same time, wiggle his wat out this dilemma without being a snitch.

Taking their seats on the metal stools. Tahira was the first to speak, "I thought you said you was home to stay?", she said with an angry face.

Caught off guard by the greeting Telly said, "You'll understand when you get older."

Snapping her head Tahira's way, Tanya gave her daughter a look as if to say "Stop it". Telly caught the look saying, "Naw, let her say what she want." Directing his eyes to Tahira he asked, "You got anything else you want to say?"

Leaning upon the edge of the concrete table, Tahira asked, "Yeah, when you coming home?"

He answered truthfully, "I don't know baby. You'll be the first to know when I do though."

Glad that he didn't go into detail, Tanya quickly changed the subject. "So how's your leg doing?"

Smiling he said, "It's alright, a little sore that's all. Thanks to that medical book you always leave lying around."

"What you talking about?"

"The pressure point stuff. I used that knowledge to stop the loss of blood."

"Oh okay. I'm glad you alright. I been missing you a lot."

"Yeah me too.", he said looking at Tanya and Tahira.

"The other day I was getting some groceries, and I happened to walk past this law firm. The same lawyers who be handling high profile cases for celebrities. On the way back I was thinking about checking with them. Unless, you got other plans for a lawyer." Waiting for a response. She noticed and understood the look he gave her. Turning towards Tahira she reached in her bra and pulled out some bills. "Here

Tahira. Go and get yourself something from the snack machine. The one I seen when we first came in."

Not really hungry, but understanding what was going on, Tahira took the money and then left out. Once the door shut behind her, Telly began in earnest. "Check this out yo. I'm just gonna keep it all the way real. That money I left ya'll is for ya'll. So you can be straight out there. Spending money on a lawyer ain't gonna do men no good. It will just be a waste."

Immediately understanding what he was getting at. Tears started to well up in her eyes. "We can still try though. You never know."

"Ain't you been watching the news? It's a wrap this time. I'm fucked up. I would be less than a man to tell you otherwise."

Tears rolling down her face now. She left herself go. Telly watching from the other side was gripped with emotions as well. He hadn't cried since he was a little kid. Now though, he felt them coming on. "Maybe we should visit some other time. Ain't no use in getting Tahira all upset. She only a baby."

Wanting to stay regardless, after driving so far to see him, understanding from the other side what he was getting at though. She said, "Yeah maybe your right. I shouldn't of brought her anyway. I just figured it would be good for her to see you. Newt time, I'll come by myself. I'll drop her off at my mothers house, and I'll be back to see you tomorrow. Is that alright? Is it safe for us to be in Philly like that?"

Wiping a single solitary tear from his face. He said in a defeated tone, "Yeah, its alright. I love you baby. Don't you ever forget that."

Wiping some of her tears away, she responded, "I love you too."

At that moment, Tahira returned with snacks in her hand. As soon as she entered the room, Telly stood up saying, "Well alright ya'll. I got to go. You take care of your mother. You hear me?"

"We just got here though.", Tahira said in disappointment.

"Yeah I know. That's how these stupid places are.", Tanya said.

"You know I love you right shortie. Don't you?"

"Umm Hmm."

"Aiight. Just making sure. Like I said earlier, when you get older you'll understand.", he said with finality. Then, he reached out and pressed a button on the wall. In less than a minute, guards quickly arrived. Blowing a kiss to each other, they parted company. Emotional pain weighing heavy on each of them equally.

Chapter 25

It was a month and a half after the arrests of the Broadie Boyz. And the Federal Detention Venter in Philly was buzzing with anticipation. Any casual observer would of thought John Gotti reincarnate was about to arrive or something. The way prisoners were carrying on and what not.

The anticipation wasn't lost on the administration either. As the transport van carrying a healed Broke arrived at the facility. He was greeted by nothing less than ten guards. Five walking on each side of him. All having their batons drawn and at the ready, even though Broke was shackled and handcuffed at all times.

Peeping out the scene as he walked in between them. Broke was a little puzzled at his reception. They were acting like he was Bruce Lee or something. Able to break out of chains and whip thirty people ass single handedly.

After walking down several corridors and through numerous doors. They finally arrived at his destination. A cell at the end of a big tier. Equipped with a commode, a metal desk, and one bunk. He only knew though, not by anything they said, but because once they reached there, they collectively started to take off his restraints.

"Control open G-28. Control open G-28.", A guard spoke into his radio.

"Ten Four"

Immediately after the cell door opened, nudged a little, they directed him into the cell. Then the same guard said, "Control close G-28."

"Ten Four"

Opening his trap door, the guards proceeded to undo his handcuffs. When they were off, they closed it back and left. Broke listened as the sounds of their boots faded. Leaving him in a momentary silence.

"Ay Broke! Broke!", somebody yelled from the tier.

"Yo!"

"What's up fam?! You alright?!"

"Who dat?"

"Man Man."

Smile breaking out at a familiar voice. After being subjected to hostility for a month and a half. By the guards at the hospital. Broke said, "What up yo?"

"Just figured I give you a proper welcome."

"Where everybody else at?"

"On lock up with us. This whole tier alone damn near nothing but fam. They say they don't want us on their yard. Might cause a riot or something."

Sporadic laughter broke out at the sound of that. Then, seconds later each member called out a greeting as well. Feeling a certain kind of comfort in being reunited with their leader. A man who had blessed each of their lives with his leadership. And whom they would each follow faithfully still.

"So what's the schedule like? Somebody give me the run down, so I can begin to adjust."

Speaking out, Man Man said, "Basically its like this. We be on twenty three hour lockdowm everyday. Only coming out for an hour a day. That's only for our recreation and shower. Canteen run is three times a week on a second shift. When we get hygiene shit and food.—-"

Interrupting him Broke said, "So what time is rec?"

"In about thirty minutes. They will come through and take us to the cages out back. That's when you'll see the rest of the family. Keno, Shock, Big Mook. They all on the other tier. Ain't but two tiers."

"Where that nigga Telly at?"

At the mention of his name, it seemed the whole tier underwent an abrupt change. The soft chatter taking place suddenly stopped like a nigga just mentioned the Devils name in the presence of God.

"He on the tier with Big Mook and em. They just let him out the infirmary about two weeks ago. Kemo tried to get at him his first night in by jamming his door during shower time. He couldn't get his shit off though. Keeping it all the way real. He couldn't handle him. You know how big Telly is. He get an A for effort though."

"No doubt", Broke cosigned.

"Since the guards be on point, they wanted to put him on the yard at first. So he could be separated from us. Then they thought better of it. Figuring he would be safer behind these doors." Pausing for a second, he went to spit in his commode. Then coming back to the door he said, "That nigga will never be safe around me. That's my word. I wish I was over there. Animal was my fucking nigga."

"He be coming out for rec?"

"Yeah, everyday. I guess the nigga trying to make it seem like he ain't scared."

"He ain't gotta be to lose his life...", Broke said in a low voice.

Walking with the sound of handcuffs jingling in their wake, the guards yelled "Tier I! Rec time! Rec time! If you ain't ready, you ain't going! So be dressed when we get to your trap!"

Sitting on his bunk tying up his black state boots. Once done, Telly slid a sharpened piece of steel on the inside. Just like everybody else, he knew Broke had just arrived. Thoughts in his mind upon hearing the news were full of all kinds of different scenarios. He be a lie if he said he wasn't scared. Still though, being scared and a bitch was two totally different things. He didn't survive in state prison without learning something.

"You ready?", a guard asked while opening up his trap.

Saying nothing, Telly just stood up, then got handcuffed and waited for his door to pop.

"Open up I-16."

As the door slid open, Telly walked out on the tier. Past vicious faces of the Broadie Boyz who slept on his tier level. Through some corridors situated at the bottom of the stairs. On out to the people on lock-up rec yard. Where instead of basketball courts and weight piles. Like it was on the population yards. It was only row upon row of cages.

The noise on the yard was loud as he entered it. Keeping to the middle and far away from the cages as he could. Telly looked around, trying to find out if Broke came out on rec or not.

On Telly's blindside watching him as he walked to his cage. Broke said just loud enough for Telly to hear. "Here I go nigga. Thought you wasn't gonna see me again didn't you?"

Turning to the familiar voice. A chill ran up his spine. As he laid eyes for the first time since that night, on the man who was somewhat responsible for the state his life was in now. Standing there staring at him with unmistakable hatred.

"Aiight Williams. Is you coming or going back?", a guard asked sarcastically.

Giving Broke a final look, Telly continued walking down to his allotted cage. Allowing the guard to take off his handcuff so he could exercise inside of it. Fifteen minutes into his rec time, suddenly he heard Broke's familiar voice again. Yelling over top of the noise of the other men.

"I thought you was a real nigga Telly!"

Turning to face him through the holes in the gate. Where he was located several cages away. Telly welcomed his opportunity for dialogue. 'I am nigga!"

"Naw you aint! Real niggas don't flip on they family for no reason."

"I had a reason. And that reason was to get out of this shit.", he said, gesturing at the cages they were in. "But I knew you wouldn't let me."

"What...you thought I was supposed to? C'mon yo. You knew what you was getting into out the gate. I made sure of it." Pausing for a brief second, he continued. "But what the fuck that got to do with stealing my money?! Didn't I make sure you had plenty of it?!"

Telly had no immediate response. He knew he was in violation. He had to come to realization a long time ago. What could he do about it now? All he could do was try to survive.

Catching the look on his face Broke said, "Yeah I figured you wouldn't have nothing to say. You know that shit was foul. Now Animal dead because of you."

Remembering that night imagining what they would have done to him, in a fit of anger Telly yelled, "Fuck Animal!!"

The emotion in his voice sent the whole yard into silence. At which time with the same amount of emotion, Broke yelled back, "Naw. Fuck you!" Then turned his back.

Laying atop his bunk on his back. Telly laid the library book he held down beside him. He couldn't concentrate no matter how hard he tried. His mind just kept drifting back to earlier on the rec yard. Remembering the pure hatred he saw in Broke's face.

For the first time since he been down, he now started to second guess himself. Asking himself if being a snitch was the smarter move or not. Who cares what people thought about him...Broke didn't even like him and was out to kill him. So why would he have declined the Agents offer of "helping himself". Telling them to go fuck themselves when they visited again. Why not cut his stay in the penal?...Then at the same time, get some sort of protection. If he helped the DA with their case, surely they would make sure he wasn't around any members of the Broadie Boyz.

In frustration, he swept the book beside him onto the floor. Sending it tumbling across his cell underneath his commode. Climbing off the bunk behind it. He started to pace in his small confines. A conflict of emotion races through his whole body.

What he was feeling was the effects of pure fear. A state of being that leaves a person confusion. He knew it was just a matter of time.

Before they managed to orchestrate another attempt on his life. Now that their "God" had arrived in the Detention Center. All his little angels were even more eager to represent.

When he was coming in from the yard. A member in one of the cages he was passing, spit through the cage in Telly's face. With a feeling of disgust Telly ran up close to the man's cage. Then in retaliation, let fly a barrage of spit. Until the guards had to come pull him away. A brief glance at where Broke stood. Made Telly even madder, upon seeing Broke doubled over in laughter.

Pulling off his white T-shirt. Telly decided to let off some steam. The way he always did on his last bid when stressed. Dropping to the floor, he proceeded to do push ups. Seventy-five a set. Welcoming the pain he felt as he worked to completion.

After several sets completed his mind got a little clearer. And he chided himself for his cowardly thoughts forty-five minutes ago. Fuck looking over his shoulder.....One, two, three, four, five...Fuck them niggas....Six, Seven, Eight, Nine, Sixty....I'm a warrior....One, Two, Three, Four, Five.....I ain't never been a bitch or on P.C.(Protective Custody)...Six, Seven, Eight, Nine, Seventy...And I never will.....One, Two, Three, Four, Seventy-Five.....Fuck it. Standing up he went and washed off the sweat.

Chapter 26

The next day Telly sat tying his boots. Getting ready once again for his time on the yard. That was the thing about prison. The routine hardly ever changes. Everything is a schedule day in and day out. Designed to make a prisoners life as mundane as possible. He could remember on his last bid. Old timers who had been down over thirty years. Forgetful of their own birthdays. So much institutionalized with prisons regular routine.

Sliding his shank down in his book. Telly stood just as the guards came in the block. Yelling across the tier the same thing they always did. Until they got to the first cell which was Telly's.

"You ready Williams?", a guard asked opening the trap.

"Can you come back to me last please. I got to use the bathroom."

"C'mon Williams. You been here long enough. You should have done that before we got here."

"C'mon Jackson. It ain't gonna inconvenience you none to come back for me this time."

Staring at him for a few seconds the guard said, "Alright, this time. But only because you don't never give me any problems. Don't make it a habit though."

"Good look yo. I appreciate it."

As the guard walked off, Telly walked down the small space of his cell. Over to his metal desk in the corner on the wall. Then grabbed up a paper clip he had sitting atop some papers. Straightened it out, he tucked it under his arm band, that all prisoners had to wear for identification. Then he went back and waited by his cell door. Thinking about what he was getting ready to do.

Fifteen minutes later. The guard came walking back saying, "Aiight Williams. You better be ready."

"Lets go", Telly said placing his hands out to be handcuffed.

"Open I-16"

Coming out, Telly walked down the empty tier. Out through the corridors that led to the rec yard. Once he was sure the guard Jackson wasn't watching anymore. He pulled out the paprrclip he had concealed. Then used it to unlock his handcuffs. A trick he learned years ago on his last bid.

Putting them back on, so they would appear to be locked, but weren't. He headed outside past the numerous cages. Scanning the yard once again for Broke's location. While heading towards the single guard responsible for lockup rec yard, standing by Telly's allotted cage.

"Good Morning Mr. Williams. I thought you probably wasn't coming out today. Your usually first.", the tall white man said.

"Yeah, I know. I just had to use the bathroom."

As soon as the guard went to open his cage, Telly suddenly swung at the guard's blindside a right hook. Connecting with his temple. Sending him bouncing off the cage and onto the concrete unconscious. The sound of his keys jiggling loudly as he fell.

Hearing the unusual noise. Everybody in the vicinity stopped what they were doing. Staring with curiosity as Telly bent down and scooped up the cage key. Dug inside his boot for his shank. Then raced back the way he came. Coming to a stop in front of Broke's cage.

Looking at Telly's sudden appearance with surprise. After getting over his initial shock. Telly pulled out a shank Man Man blessed him with the other night. "Well what you waiting on nigga?" Open the gate so I can slay your bitch ass", he said showing no fear.

Not expecting Broke to have a shank too when he planned the situation last night. Cautiously Telly placed the key in the lock and turned. Before he could even pull the gate open, Broke kicked it open for him. Then within seconds he was already out the cage. Making a lunge for Telly's midsection holding his shank underhanded.

Backing out the way. Telly was too off balance to counterattack. So he just side stepped as Broke's swing caught nothing but air. He reacted a little quicker though. When Broke made another lunge. This time he swung his shank, cutting Broke's cheek open as simultaneously Broke caught him too, penetrating his stomach just enough to cause bleeding.

"That's for Animal bitch!", somebody yelled from one of the cages. Both men coming apart a few feet. They analyzed each other looking for an opening. Already out of breath, Telly took the brief respite to switch his grip on his shank to overhand. So as to allow himself the freedom to throw punches as well.

Immediately seeing the advantage in this particular grip also. Broke followed suit almost instantly. Then with no hesitation whatsoever he quickly threw a jab with the hand holding the shank. Catching Telly on the jaw soundly. Then came down on Telly's collarbone with the shank, creating a puncture wound near Telly's left shoulder.

Spinning out the way as Broke came down on another swing from the shank, Telly let loose with two hard hooks to Broke's temple, causing him to stumble from the force of the blows. Then coming in low while Broke was off balance. Telly football tackled Broke to the ground. Then with lighting speed, he started stabbing Broke numerous times in his torso and neck, sending blood spraying everywhere at one time.

With every swing Telly felt a rush. Every drop of blood that splattered on his face seemed to be a release from the stress that he endured by being associated with Broke. Broadie Boyz that were watching, suddenly in anger started kicking their cages wildly. Trying as hard as they could to bend the lock on their cage so they could come to their leaders aid.

Hearing the loud noise from his perch inside the gun tower, a black guard stepped out the hooch to investigate with his Mini Assault Rifle. Looking down on the rec yard for the cause of disturbance. Slowly scanning in between the cages until he saw his coworker, lying unconscious beside an open cage. Grabbing his radio, he quickly called for help. "Officer down segregation rec yard! Officer down segregation rec yard!"

Frantically looking around now, he jacked a round up in the firing chamber. When Telly and Broke came into his field of vision. Treating the situation as a potential riot, he fired a warning shot yelling, "Put the knife down and get on the ground!!"

Hearing the gunshot, Telly got up with the knife still in hand, looking down in a daze at the mess left of Broke. He was in such a state of rage, he didn't even remember doing what he did. Standing with a look of confusion on his face, he stared at Broke laying there dead with multiple wounds all over. Puncture wounds in the fifties.

Seeing Telly's failure to adhere to the warning shot and order, the guard aimed the assault rifle squarely at Telly's body. Then let out two shots. The force slammed the unsuspecting Telly to the ground. Spraying his guts all across the ground.

As he hit the ground gasping for air. For a few seconds, he was finally free. Free from the clutches of a bad decision. A decision that got him involved in something he wasn't built for. If only he knew.......That was the last thought he had before he died.

www.ingramcontent.com/pod-product-compliance
Lightning Source LLC
Chambersburg PA
CBHW061447150726
47987CB00001B/362